"I believe you have something of mine,"

Brice began.

"Something of yours?" Eve looked at him blankly, noting how the rain plastered down his hair, making his bold features more vivid. *Get a grip, girl,* she chided herself, her heart pounding in unsteady rhythm.

He looked down, making her realize he held a laundry basket in his arm. "Yes, and I believe these are yours." He gestured to the top item in the basket, which happened to be a pair of her white, cotton, no-nonsense panties. His eyes held an indecent twinkle of light that caused the blood to leave her face, then rush back with volcanic force.

For a single, wild moment, she wanted to vehemently deny that the boring, plain underwear were hers. For some crazy reason, she wanted him to believe she was prone to black lace and red ribbons, garter belts and sexy chemises.

The craziness fled as quickly as it had appeared.

Dear Reader,

June . . . a month of courtship and romance, white lace and wedding vows. And at Silhouette Romance we're celebrating those June brides and grooms with some very special tales of love and marriage. Best of all—YOU'RE INVITED!

As every bride knows, you can't march down the aisle without the essentials, starting with *Something Old*—a fun-filled look at love with an older man—from Toni Collins. Gabriella Thorne falls for her boss, Adrian Lacross—a handsome and oh-so-charming . . . vampire. Can the love of a good woman change Adrian's fly-by-night romantic ways?

Something New was in store for prim-and-proper Eve Winthrop the day the new high school principal came to town. Carla Cassidy brings us the *irresistible* Brice Maxwell, who shakes up a sleepy Oklahoma town and dares Eve to take a walk on the wild side.

Linda Varner brings us *Something Borrowed* from the magical land of Oz! A tornado whisked Brooke Brady into Patrick Sawyer's life. Is handsome Patrick really a heartless Tin Man—or Brooke's very own heart's desire?

Something Blue is an unexpected little package from the stork for newly divorced Teddy Falco and Quinn Barnett. Jayne Addison's heartwarming style lends special magic to this story of a couple reunited by the miracle of their new baby.

Elizabeth August gives the final touch to our wedding bouquet with *Lucky Penny*. Celina Warley and Reid Prescott weren't looking for a marriage with love, but with luck, would love find them?

Our FABULOUS FATHERS series continues with an unforgettable hero and dad—Judd Tanner, in *One Man's Vow* by Diana Whitney. Judd is a devoted father who will go the limit to protect his four children—even if it means missing out on the love of one very special woman.

In the months to come look for books by more of your favorite authors—Annette Broadrick, Diana Palmer, Lucy Gordon, Suzanne Carey and many more.

Until then, happy reading!

Anne Canadeo
Senior Editor

SOMETHING NEW
Carla Cassidy

Silhouette
ROMANCE™
Published by Silhouette Books New York
America's Publisher of Contemporary Romance

To John Cook, a dedicated principal
and a terrific dad!

SILHOUETTE BOOKS
300 East 42nd St., New York, N.Y. 10017

SOMETHING NEW

Copyright © 1993 by Carla Bracale

ISBN: 0-373-08942-2

First Silhouette Books printing June 1993

Printed in the U.S.A.

Books by Carla Cassidy

Silhouette Romance

Patchwork Family #818
Whatever Alex Wants... #856
Fire and Spice #884
Homespun Hearts #905
Golden Girl #924
Something New #942

Silhouette Desire

A Fleeting Moment #784

Silhouette Shadows

Swamp Secrets #4

CARLA CASSIDY

Fourteen years ago, Carla Cassidy walked down the aisle to wed her "Brice." Much of her wedding day passed in a haze.... She doesn't remember the kind of flowers she had, she doesn't remember the music. What she does remember is the look in his eyes as she approached...it was the look of love, and it's kept her happily married ever since.

Brice Maxwell on marriage:

Marriage to the right woman would be like riding a good motorcycle on a long stretch of road...comfort and security, but with the exhilaration of the wind in your face.

Eve Winthrop on marriage:

You've got to be kidding. With a crazy sister and a demanding mother to take care of, the last thing I need is a husband. I'd never make it through all that laundry.

Dog on marriage:

Woof!

Chapter One

Never cut your hair when you're angry or upset. Eve Winthrop wished somebody had given her that advice thirty minutes earlier, when she had picked up a pair of scissors and begun snipping. What had begun as a little trim job had turned into a scalping of mammoth proportions.

She now stared at her reflection in the mirror with horror, noticing how her dark hair stuck up in uneven spikes all over her head. Good grief, what had she done? She looked like an overage punk rocker.

She jumped when the doorbell rang. Still dazed by the havoc she'd wreaked on her hair, she went to answer the door, scissors still clutched in her hand.

The first thing she noticed about the man who stood on her doorstep was that he had dark hair—lots of it.

It was sinfully long, much longer than her own, with just a hint of curl at the shoulders. She instantly coveted it.

"Is this the duplex for rent?" His voice was a low rumble, like thunder in the distance. She thought she detected an East Coast accent.

His voice snapped her out of her worship of his hair and she instantly noticed other things about his physical appearance. Like the fact that his eyes were the clearest blue she'd ever seen, and his upper torso looked powerfully fit beneath the black leather jacket he wore like a second skin. His face was chiseled in lines and planes that spoke of hard living. A dimple in each cheek tempered the look of harshness.

Realizing he was waiting for her answer, she flushed. "Uh, no, it's right next door," she said, pointing with the scissors to the door next to hers.

He grinned at her. It was a sexy, laid-back grin that instantly sent a shiver of indecent tingles up Eve's spine. He gestured to her hair. "Did you do that on purpose, or did you get your head too close to a food processor?"

"I beg your pardon?" She looked at him quizzically, sure she must have misunderstood.

"If that's the style you're going to sport, you definitely need something more updated in your clothing." His brilliant eyes perused her from head to toe, making her feel as if her comfortable cotton blouse had just turned transparent and her tailored slacks had shrunk three sizes.

"What's wrong with my clothes?" she demanded, affronted by his outspoken rudeness. "I think you're impertinent."

"Impertinent?" He threw back his head and laughed, exposing gleaming white teeth. "You sound like an old-maid schoolteacher."

Eve gathered herself up to her full five-foot-three and glared at him icily. "I am a schoolteacher."

His forehead wrinkled, causing his dark eyebrows to dance upwards with curiosity. "But are you an old maid?"

"That, sir, is none of your business." With that, she slammed the door, half hoping she'd catch the end of his brash nose with it.

Imagine the nerve of the man, she thought as she stormed back to her place in front of her bathroom mirror. She hoped Mr. Williams, her landlord, was smart enough not to rent the other side of the duplex to the rude man. That was all she needed, a leather-clad, outspoken, obnoxious devil as a neighbor. As if her life weren't complicated enough all ready.

"Speaking of complications..." She stared at her reflection once again. There was no way around it, she was going to have to make a trip to her beautician to repair the damage. She snatched up the telephone and within minutes had her appointment. As she stepped outside her front door, Mr. Williams and the leather-bound buffoon walked out the other door.

"Ah, Miss Winthrop, I'd like you to meet your new neighbor," Mr. Williams said.

"We met earlier," she replied, refusing to look at the man who, it seemed, would soon be living next door to her. She pasted a smile on her face for her landlord's benefit. Her smile wavered when she saw the huge motorcycle that sat in the driveway. It looked like some menacing monster, with its gleaming chrome parts and its gas tank painted the colors of billowing fire.

She shot a glare at its owner, again noticing his leather jacket. If there was a grinning skull, or something similar, painted on his back, then she was definitely going to raise a ruckus with Mr. Williams. She would not live next door to a member of some biker gang.

"Uh, please excuse me... I've got an appointment," she said, hurrying to where her car was parked out by the curb. Feeling those azure eyes on her backside, she quickened her pace, grateful when she slid into the confines of the car.

"Honey, I've told you and told you...when you need a little trim, give me a call, but don't pick up the scissors," Kathy Blakemore exclaimed as she worked to repair the damage to Eve's hair.

Eve smiled remorsefully. "Don't worry. I think I've learned my lesson."

"Ha! That's what I heard the last time," Kathy retorted, spraying untangling solution and combing down the dark spikes. "You only do this sort of thing when you're really upset. What has Colleen managed to do this time?''

Eve grimaced at the thought of her younger sister. "I spent last night bailing her out of jail." Eve waited for Kathy's gasp of astonishment, then continued. "Four outstanding parking tickets, and two speeding. There was a bench warrant out, and she got pulled over for driving with expired tags."

"You should have let her stay in jail. Maybe that would teach her a lesson," Kathy returned, moving around to work on the front of Eve's hair.

"I couldn't do that. Mom would have a tizzy fit. She still thinks of Colleen as her baby."

Kathy snorted. "A twenty-three-year-old isn't a baby."

"At least she finally has a job she seems to like."

"Well, that's a step in the right direction." Kathy paused a moment to snip uncomfortably close to Eve's ear, then continued. "So, how's your love life?"

"Love life? What's that?" Eve sighed. "I don't have time for romance."

"That's because you're too busy cleaning up everyone else's messes." Kathy paused a moment to unwrap a piece of bubble gum and pop it into her mouth, then reached up and patted her own elaborately arranged bottle-red hair. "So, no exciting men on the scene?"

Eve shook her head, irritated that the first vision that popped into her mind was of her motorcycle-driving new neighbor in his deliciously tight jeans.

With his wicked eyes and grin, he'd been attractive, in a sort of primal, hard-edged kind of way. Definitely not Eve's type. She frowned, depressed to realize that at twenty-nine she had yet to figure out exactly what her type was.

"How are things going at school?"

Eve frowned once again. "A real mess. Mr. Stevens has been gone almost two months, and the whole school is starting to fall apart. A school without a principal is like a country without a government—total chaos."

"When is the new guy supposed to start?"

Eve shrugged. "In the next couple of days. I'm really not sure. I missed the teachers' meeting when they announced everything."

"Think this one will last?"

"If he can please the school board."

"You mean if he can please that old windbag Mrs. Worthington. She owns the school board. She runs the whole show."

Eve remained silent, having learned long ago not to comment on the longstanding political situation of Mrs. Worthington and the school board. Besides, the job her sister had just gotten was as the woman's secretary. She wasn't about to say anything that might get back to Mrs. Worthington and somehow jeopardize her sister's job.

Kathy popped a bubble from her wad of gum, then stepped back to look at her efforts. "I'm going to have to leave this hair on top sort of spiked up. There's not much else I can do with the length you left me. At least you have the bone structure to wear your hair so short." She twirled Eve's chair around so that Eve, too, could view the end result.

Eve studied her reflection critically. Now that the initial shock had worn off and Kathy had worked a little magic, she realized that her hair didn't look half-bad. Kathy was right—the cropped cut did emphasize her large green eyes and high cheekbones.

"My students will think it's awesome," she exclaimed, thinking of the reaction of her high school English pupils when she returned to work on Monday. "Thanks, Kathy. I appreciate you working me in on such short notice," Eve said as the redhead unwound the plastic covering from around her neck.

"What are best friends for?" Kathy smiled at her. "Call me next weekend. Maybe we can catch a movie or something."

Eve nodded. Then, after paying for the trim, she left the beauty shop.

The air was perfumed with the sweet scent of spring flowers as she leisurely made her way back to where she'd parked the car. Everywhere she looked, signs of spring beckoned her to take the day off, go to the park, enjoy the rebirth of the earth after winter's long grasp. The small town of Pawkinah, Oklahoma, was gorgeous in the spring, before the summer duststorms transformed everything into a monotonous brown.

Eve would have liked to linger, but she'd promised her mother she'd come over and help her with income taxes, and she'd assured Colleen the night before that she'd contact her lawyer about representing Colleen in court. Besides, she had a stack of English papers to grade at home, and she was a firm believer in work coming before pleasure.

With a deep sigh, she got back into her car and headed for her mother's house, grateful there wasn't a pair of scissors around, because she had another overwhelming urge to cut her hair.

"I've got to do something about my social life," Eve muttered later that night as she sat in a plastic chair in the laundry facility for the duplexes, watching her laundry tumbling around and around in a clothes dryer.

A Saturday night, and here she sat, her biggest excitement the anticipation of discovering if her new stirrup pants would retain their size or shrink to Barbie doll proportions.

At least she wasn't the only one finding laundry a way to pass a Saturday night. Two other dryers whirled around, attesting to the fact that there were other lonely souls in the six duplexes. Somehow that didn't make her feel any better.

Most of the time she wasn't bothered by the lack of social stimuli in her life. She was usually either too busy or too tired to notice. But there were occasional moments of solitude that produced vague longings, stirrings of loneliness. There were times when she wished for someone special in her life, a man who would share her hopes and dreams.

Why couldn't somebody wonderful move in next door? Perhaps a single doctor or lawyer looking for a sedate schoolteacher as a wife? Her face darkened as she thought of her new neighbor.

He'd spent the afternoon moving in his belongings. Eve had stood at her window, watching him, wondering why she found him repellent and fascinating at the same time. He positively oozed sexual appeal, as well as a sort of savage spiritual freedom.

As he'd worked, unloading a small rental truck full of furnishings, he'd shrugged out of his leather jacket, exposing powerful shoulders and lean hips. She supposed there were some women who would be titillated by his overt maleness, but she certainly wasn't one of them. Still, she'd stood at the window an indecently long time, unable to tear her gaze away from him.

A clap of thunder boomed overhead, making her jump in surprise. Apparently the threatening clouds that had hung aloft all evening had finally managed to produce a spring storm.

"Damn." She got up out of her chair and moved over to the door, blinking as a bolt of lightning danced across the sky, as if showing off its tremendous power. Seconds later, thunder rumbled again, chastising the wayward lightning.

Terrific. Just what she needed. This laundry dungeon for the renters of the duplexes was dreary enough without the benefit of a storm.

Another flash of lightning exploded, this one so close she could have sworn she heard it sizzle. The power went off. The room was plunged into darkness . . . and there was complete silence.

For a long moment, she stood still, waiting to see if the electricity would be restored. Seconds ticked by, and nothing happened. Peering outside, she saw that the entire neighborhood was in darkness. Sighing irritably, she made her way to the row of dryers, hampered in her movements by the utter darkness of the room.

"At least they're almost dry," she muttered as she shoved her clothes into a laundry bag. She hefted the bag over her shoulder and ran for her duplex, hoping the rain would hold off long enough for her to get inside.

She made it to her porch before the first raindrops began falling. Fumbling with her keys, she opened the door and stumbled inside, breathing a sigh of relief when she heard the rain begin to pelt the windows in earnest.

Minutes later, candles burning on her table to provide a modicum of light and changed into comfortable pajamas, Eve sat on her sofa. "Hi, Fluffy," she said to her white cat, who jumped up on her lap and purred a greeting. "What's the matter, does the storm bother you?" she asked as the cat lowered her head and rubbed against Eve's stomach, meowing plaintively.

Eve eyed the stack of student papers on the table. "They can wait until tomorrow," she muttered, not willing to strain her eyes grading papers by candle-light.

As she sat there, scratching the cat behind her ears, her thoughts went once again to her new neighbor. What kind of a job did a man like that have? Mechanic? Collection-agency employee? Armed robber?

She smiled at her own fanciful thoughts. If it were two hundred years ago and Pawkinah were a coastal town, she'd believe her new neighbor to be a pirate. With his long hair and rakish air, it was easy to imagine him sailing the high seas, pirating loot and stealing women's hearts.

She frowned at the last thought. Apparently she'd been reading too many historical romances—her one secret indulgence. Pirate, indeed. He was just a long-haired lowlife with an arrogant air and a brash mouth. Certainly not the type of man who warranted her interest or her thoughts.

She gently pushed the cat off her lap and stood up. The one thing she could do in the semidarkness was fold her laundry. She reached for the duffel bag and pulled out the first item.

A pair of jeans, still slightly damp—and definitely not hers. "Oh, no," she murmured, dumping the bag's contents on the sofa and staring at them in dismay. In the darkness of the laundry room, she must have loaded the contents of the wrong dryer into her bag.

She started to shove the clothes back, then hesitated, hearing the sound of the rain relentlessly pounding the roof. She certainly wasn't going to wade out in that mess to exchange the clothes. She'd wait until the rain stopped, or at least slowed. In the meantime, she might as well fold these clothes so that the owner wouldn't have to take an iron to everything.

She picked up the jeans again. They were men's jeans—waist about thirty-two... length about thirty-four.... Tall and lean, she mused, clothespinning the damp pants at the waist to a hanger. She hung them on an arm of her floor lamp, where they seemed to stand at attention, just waiting for a pair of muscular legs to fill them out.

It wasn't until she picked up a black T-shirt that she realized whose clothes she was folding. He'd worn the very same shirt when he'd unloaded the rental truck that afternoon. She folded the shirt, trying not to think of how his broad shoulders had neatly filled out every inch of the material.

She felt a warm blush sweep over her face as she picked up a pair of briefs. No plain white Fruit-of-the-Loom for Mr. Macho. He wore colored bikinis that were certainly sexier than anything Eve owned.

As she finished folding the rest of the clothes, she was disturbed by visions of how he'd look wearing those indecent little briefs.

His stomach would be flat and well-toned.... His chest would be broad, and covered with just enough hair to make it a tactile pleasure.... His legs would be long and well muscled....

Eve jumped and emitted a small scream when thunder rumbled overhead at the same time a sharp knock sounded on her door.

Hurrying to the door, wondering who would venture out on such a night, she cracked it open and gasped as her gaze locked with the brilliant blue eyes of the man who had just occupied her thoughts.

"What do you want?" she asked inanely, catching her breath as lightning crackled, backlighting him so that he looked like a presence from another world—which was exactly what he was to Eve.

"I believe you have something of mine," he said.

"Something of yours?" Eve looked at him blankly, noting how the rain plastered his hair to his scalp, making his bold features more vivid. Get a grip, girl, she chided herself, her heart pounding in an unsteady rhythm.

He looked down, making her realize he held a laundry basket in his arm. "Yes, and I believe these are yours." He gestured to the top item in the basket, which happened to be a pair of her no-nonsense white cotton panties. His eyes held an indecent twinkle of light that caused the blood to leave her face, then rush back with volcanic force.

For a single wild moment, she wanted to deny vehemently that the boring plain underwear were hers. For some crazy reason she wanted him to believe that she was prone to black lace and red ribbons, garter belts and sexy chemises. The craziness fled as quickly as it had appeared.

"Oh, uh...come in...." She stepped back, allowing him to sweep into the living room. Immediately the room seemed to shrink as it filled with his overwhelming presence. It was his blatant masculinity that threw her. In her world of education, she was accustomed to men who wore suits and ties. The men in her world didn't wear jeans that stuck to their legs with familiarity. They didn't wear T-shirts that exposed firm forearms and a rock-hard chest. And they definitely weren't the kind of men who wore colored bikini briefs. Again her face suffused with heat.

"Where do you want these?" He gestured to the clothes basket in his hands.

"Oh, you can just dump them there on the sofa." She indicated the spot where Fluffy had sat before the knock on the door sent her scurrying for the safe darkness of the kitchen. "How—how did you know they were mine?"

He dumped the clothing on the sofa, then turned and looked at her, his eyes amused as they made a slow journey from the top of her head to the tip of her toes. "Everything is extremely sensible, and you strike me as the sensible type. Besides—" he picked up a lightweight windbreaker "—your name is stenciled in the collar of this."

Eve nodded, wondering why, when he'd said she struck him as a sensible woman, it had sounded almost like an insult. What was wrong with being sensible? "I apologize for the mix-up. The power went off in the laundry room, and I couldn't see, and I guess I emptied the wrong dryer by mistake." Eve knew she was rambling, but she couldn't seem to stop herself. "It was dark, and I couldn't see."

"No problem." He shrugged and helped her get his clothing together. He turned to leave, but paused at her front door, a devilish grin on his sexy mouth. "Did you know that in the candlelight your pajamas are almost transparent?" With a blatant wink, he disappeared out into the storm.

Eve looked down, gasping when she realized he was right. Her proper, tailored pajamas were less than proper with the light from the candles flickering behind her. How rude of him to comment on it! Did the man have no manners at all? No sense of propriety? How was she ever going to survive living next to the man?

Brice Maxwell placed the basket of clothes on his kitchen table, then sat down in the overstuffed recliner that sat near the picture window. He stared out at the storm outside, a small smile playing over his features.

"Hey, Dog," he said as his rottweiler greeted him, pushing his massive head beneath Brice's hand. Brice petted the dog absently, his thoughts still on the woman next door.

The moment he'd first seen her, when she'd answered her door with a pair of scissors in her hand and her hair sticking up helter-skelter, a chord of harmony had been strummed deep inside Brice's chest.

She had practically vibrated with tension, and her eyes had radiated a frustration with life. She'd looked at him as if he were the creature from the black lagoon. But, beneath the curiosity, despite her apparent aversion, Brice had felt the magic of chemistry working, hormones responding.

Eve Winthrop... the landlord had been full of information regarding Brice's neighbor. A committed teacher, a devoted daughter, a supportive sister... a pillar of the community. "An old-fashioned, proper lady, that one," Mr. Williams had said.

But Brice had seen something much different.

Eve... The perpetrator of original sin. The mother of mankind. With eyes the color of the grassy earth, and lips the red of life, Eve Winthrop could make a man think of sin.

Brice got up out of his chair and moved to the window, Dog a shadow at his heels.

He'd been worried when he decided to take a job as principal of the high school in a tiny town.

He was a New York City boy, born and bred. This move to the tiny Oklahoma town had been a culture shock in more ways than one. Eve... He thought of her again, wondering if she taught at the high school. If she did, how would she react to having him not only as a neighbor, but as a boss, as well?

He grinned to himself. He'd wondered how he would adapt to life in a small western town. He'd been afraid he'd be bored, unstimulated. But he had a feeling that, with a neighbor like Eve, boredom would be the least of his problems. And at the moment he was definitely stimulated.

Chapter Two

"Have you seen him yet?" Margie Keller, the art teacher, said when she met Eve the following Monday morning at the front door of Geoffrey Worthington High School.

"Seen who?" Eve asked curiously, shifting the stack of paperwork she carried from one arm to the other.

"Brice Maxwell, that's who..." Margie lowered her voice as Dwayne Hilton, the PE teacher, passed them with a cheery salute.

"The new principal? How could I have seen him? I just got here!" Eve exclaimed, turning into her classroom.

Margie followed behind her and parked her plump bottom on top of Eve's desk. "Wait until you see him. He's to die for. He doesn't look like any principal I've ever seen before. He's got the most gorgeous blue eyes, and long, dark hair...."

"And he wears colored bikini underwear," Eve murmured, with a sense of dread.

"I beg your pardon?" Margie looked at her in surprise.

"Oh, never mind," Eve returned, feeling the warmth of a blush steal across her face. Surely she was jumping to conclusions. There was no way Irene Worthington would hire a man like her new neighbor as principal of the school.

"Anyway, if I wasn't already married, I'd jump Brice Maxwell's bones in a flat second." Margie reached up and twirled a strand of her bright blond hair, her smile wistful, as if the very thought of jumping the man's bones was too exquisite to release. "Oh, well." She sighed and scooted off the desk. "I'd better get things organized in my room. I'm having the kids do origami today. No telling what disgusting shapes they'll manage to discover paper can be folded into." She headed for the door. "Oh, by the way, I love your new hairdo." With a backhand wave, she disappeared down the hallway.

Eve spent the next few minutes getting herself organized for the day and trying to still the thudding of her heart that had begun the moment Margie described the new principal. It was ridiculous, wasn't it, to assume that Brice Maxwell and her new neighbor were the same man? Yet she knew it wasn't so ridiculous. In fact, it was a reasonable assumption to make.

Pawkinah was a very small town, and there just weren't any to-die-for men with blue eyes and long, dark hair—except the one who'd moved in next door to her.

So what's the big deal? she asked herself as she sharpened the pencils that would be needed for the day. What difference did it make to her if her neighbor was Brice Maxwell, the new principal?

But it did make a difference. There was something about the man that disturbed her in a strange, provocative way. It was one thing to live beside him. It was quite another to work with him every day.

"Attention, teachers . . ." The intercom hissed and crackled as the voice of Ann Compton, the school secretary, filled the room. "There will be a brief meeting in the lounge in fifteen minutes. Attendance is mandatory." The intercom crackled again, then was silent.

A few minutes later, as Eve made her way to the teachers' lounge, Margie fell into step beside her. "I can't wait to see your reaction when you see him." She giggled with excitement. "I can't wait to see Mrs. Worthington's face."

"She hasn't met him yet?" Eve asked, frowning, as Margie shook her head. "Then how did she hire him?"

"You know Mrs. Worthington. She didn't want to part with the bucks to have him sent here for an interview, so she hired him sight unseen. Ann told me the man has quite an impressive résumé, and Mrs.

Worthington knows his family, who are quite promi-
nent in New York.'' Margie giggled again. ''But I have
a feeling Brice Maxwell isn't exactly what Mrs.
Worthington had in mind.''

Even though Eve was half expecting it, it was still a
shock when they entered the lounge and she saw him
standing there. He was leaning against the Coke machine, deep in conversation with Jeff Parker, the
school counselor.

''Tell me he isn't something,'' Margie whispered,
nudging Eve with an elbow.

Oh, he was something, all right—she just wasn't
sure what. At least he had taken a stab at convention,
shedding his motorcycle jacket in favor of a peach-
colored suit coat over gray trousers. Still, his white
shirt was unbuttoned at the neck, and there was no
evidence of a tie. His hair hadn't been neatly cut, but
it was pulled back with a rubber band. And nothing
spoke more eloquently of the man's alien nature than
the fact that he wore leather loafers without socks.
Without socks, for crying out loud! No man in
Pawkinah wore fancy loafers sans socks.

The most interesting thing was that he wore the look
comfortably, as if he wasn't aware that everyone in the
room was staring at him like he'd just dropped out of
the sky.

At that moment, he glanced up, and his gaze locked
with hers. A devilish light, a spark of humor, danced
in the blue depths of his eyes. A smile lifted the cor-

ners of his mouth, an intimate grin that said he knew what kind of underwear she wore.

Eve felt a blush start in the pit of her stomach and spread its warmth throughout her entire body. She fought an insane impulse to turn and run as he excused himself to Jeff and approached her, that naughty smile still teasing his lips.

"Hello, Eve," he said, his slight accent making her name sound strange and exotic.

Eve was vaguely aware of Margie's blond eyebrows almost shooting off her forehead as they tilted up in surprise.

"Mr. Maxwell," Eve returned stiffly.

"Your hair looks terrific," he observed, his smile that of someone sharing an inside joke.

"My beautician specializes in food-processor therapy," she replied, self-consciously running her hand through her shorn hair. "You could have told me who you were," she admonished, unable to keep her self-righteous ire to herself.

"I guess it just didn't cross my mind while we were exchanging clothing the other night."

Eve gasped, and Margie hiccuped in shocked surprise. "I can explain," Eve said to her friend, glaring at Brice, who seemed to be enjoying her loss of composure. He grinned innocently, as if unaware that he'd just given the rumor mill enough gossip material to last the next month. Before he had a chance to do any more damage, the entire room fell silent as an elderly woman walked in. Mrs. Irene Worthington had arrived.

The old woman entered with the dignity of a queen. Her gaze swept around the room, her dark eyes probing, assessing. When she spied Brice, her nostrils flared slightly, her mask of sociability slipping, to be replaced by a look of extreme displeasure. She recovered quickly, and the mask was firmly back in place when she approached him.

"Eve...Margie..." She greeted the two women with an imperious nod. "And you must be Brice Maxwell. I wanted to come by this morning and welcome you." She held out a hand to him. "I'd like to speak with you later this morning. I think it's important that you understand the school board's philosophies and goals as soon as possible."

Brice released her hand. Eve noticed that the teasing light was gone from his eyes. When he smiled at Mrs. Worthington, his expression was pleasant but distant. "I'm afraid it will be impossible today. With it being my first day, I'm going to be much too busy for philosophical discussions of any kind. Perhaps we could meet first thing in the morning." He offered her another pleasant smile. "Now, if you'll excuse me, I'd better get this meeting underway."

Eve saw the flare of enmity in Mrs. Worthington's eyes, the slight curl of her upper lip that spoke of anger.

"Wow," Margie breathed softly as both Brice and Mrs. Worthington moved to the front of the room. "I guess Mr. Maxwell isn't going to be one of Mrs. Worthington's puppets on a string.''

"He won't last a month." Eve made the prophecy with assurance, somehow relieved at the thought.

Minutes later, she wasn't so sure. As Brice introduced himself to his new staff of teachers and began talking about his vision for the remainder of this year and the next school year, a ripple of excitement raced through the group.

Despite Eve's personal misgivings about him, she couldn't help but respond to the challenge he issued to each and every one of them, to be the best, to devote themselves to the task of stimulating and teaching the young people of Pawkinah. He spoke of commitment, his words reminding Eve of all the reasons that had led her to choose the teaching profession years before.

"I feel the coming of change," Margie commented moments later, as she and Eve headed back to their classrooms.

"That's probably the understatement of the day," Eve returned dryly.

"You know, I haven't forgotten that little remark about you and our new principal exchanging clothing." Margie shot her an arch glance. "And I'm most anxious to hear your explanation. How about we go for a quick cup of coffee after school, and you can spill the whole sordid story?''

"There's no sordid story to spill," Eve protested. "And I can't go for coffee this afternoon. Mom invited Colleen and me over to dinner this evening, which means I need to get there early enough to cook whatever it is Mom is serving."

"I'm not letting you off the hook. Sooner or later you're going to have to explain to me what's going on between you and Brice Maxwell."

"Nothing...absolutely nothing is going on between us." Eve flushed, realizing that her voice had risen a full octave in protest. The last thing she wanted was to leave Margie with the impression that she had something going on with Brice. Margie was sort of like a sieve. Anything you poured into her sooner or later leaked out.

"Oh, gotta run!" Margie exclaimed when the bell rang and the halls immediately began to fill. Eve dismissed all thoughts of Brice Maxwell as she greeted her first-hour students.

Eve moved briskly down the sidewalk, hoping that if she walked fast enough she could outrun the irritation that prickled at her scalp.

Twilight claimed her surroundings, painting Main Street in golden hues that were much kinder than the glare of the afternoon sun. Still, even the ethereal lighting couldn't lift Eve's somber mood and aggravation.

It seemed to her that the more she did for her mother and sister, the more they required from her. She couldn't remember exactly when it had begun, when the roles had shifted and Eve had become the parent of two. It seemed lately that more and more of her time and energy was being used taking care of her mother and Colleen. There were times when she felt smothered by the responsibility and the demands. Tonight was definitely one of those times.

She'd arrived at her mom's house just in time to help get the meal on the table, her work accompanied by a litany of complaints from her mother. Violet Winthrop was a petite sixty-year-old woman with huge blue eyes and an aura of helplessness that never failed to stir a surge of guilt in Eve. "I'm so lonely." "You don't come to see me often enough." "I need to go to the grocery store more than once a week." "Can't you take me out to eat more often?"

The list went on and on, the droning buzz of a queen bee stating her desires, knowing they would all eventually be met.

Then Colleen had arrived, and the list of demands had continued, culminating in Eve loaning her sister not only another fifty dollars, but also her car for the next couple of days.

"Mrs. Worthington told me I'm going to be running a lot of errands for her this week, and you know my car isn't tagged right. I can't afford another ticket, and I don't want to lose this job," she had explained.

Nor did Eve want Colleen to lose the job. Faced with a choice between walking the eight blocks to and from school for the next couple of days and supporting Colleen because she was jobless again, Eve had opted to walk.

The only good thing that had come from the night was the gossip Colleen had spewed concerning Mrs. Worthington's reaction to Brice Maxwell. "She was appalled." Colleen had giggled. "She knew he would be somewhat unusual. She knew he used some unorthodox methods at the school where he worked back in New York. But she didn't expect all that hair.... She says there's no way he comes from the same blood as the Maxwells she knows. She says he's either adopted or a pod person."

Eve now grimed at this thought, feeling some of her tension ebb. Yes, she could see how Mrs. Worthington would think Brice was a pod person from some sort of alien plant species. Pawkinah, Oklahoma, was a town of pickup trucks and good old boys. A man like Brice Maxwell, with his flashy motorcycle and his unconventional looks, was definitely out of sync.

She sighed in relief as she turned down her block, anxious to get home and get some work done. She stopped short as she reached the end of her driveway, squinting in disbelief as she saw what sat on her front porch.

It was a dog...the ugliest one Eve had ever seen. Its head was huge, seeming to overwhelm its squat, powerful body. Missing half an ear and more than a few tufts of his black fur, the dog looked as if it had seen more than its share of battles, and lost most of them.

The animal sat directly in front of her door, making it impossible for her to enter.

She walked cautiously toward the animal, and paused when he growled menacingly. "Go away," she ordered, waving her hands to frighten him. He didn't frighten. He didn't even flinch. He merely stared at her with devil eyes, intensifying the guttural growl.

"Shoo," she hissed, eyeing the creature angrily. Of all the porches in town, why had this mutt chosen to sit sentry on hers? All she wanted to do was go inside, make herself a nice, hot cup of tea and try to unwind. It galled her that the only thing standing between her and her desires was a hostile dog missing half his ear.

How did one go about moving a dog who appeared unwilling to move? Eve didn't have a clue, especially considering the fact that the dog looked distinctly territorial. The problem was, it was her territory.

"Go home," she cried, her frustration reaching new heights. "Go away!"

At that moment, the door next to hers opened. "Dog," Brice said.

"Thank you, Mr. Maxwell, I know what it is. What I'd like to know is whose it is." Eve's voice was sarcastic. Her irritation was spilling over onto the nearest available person—him.

"No, his name is Dog, and he belongs to me." Brice stepped outside his door, bringing with him the scent of minty soap and rain-sweet shampoo. He was shirtless, exposing a firmly-muscled torso and an expanse of dark chest hair. He wore his jeans slung low over his lean hips, like a gunslinger wearing Colts for a gunfight.

For a moment, Eve forgot why she was standing there. All her family irritations, the dog keeping her out of her house...everything flew out of her head. She was caught up in an overwhelming desire to reach out and touch the wide expanse of his chest. The skin looked so soft, but she knew there would be an underlying strength of hard muscle. She tried to imagine how it would feel to dance her fingers through that hair, which formed a valentinelike pattern. She wondered how his chest would feel against her own, wondered how his strong arms would feel wrapped tightly around her.

"Eve?"

His voice snapped her back from her fantasy. She flushed, irritated that his ugly dog still sat before her front door, but even angrier than the sight of his bare skin had sparked such uncharacteristic crazy visions. What was wrong with her? Had Kathy not only trimmed her hair, but cut out some of her brain matter, as well?

"That dog should be on a leash," she exclaimed stiffly. "He looks mean."

"He's not mean, he's just misunderstood," Brice replied. He whistled softly, and the dog immediately jumped up and moved to his side, seeming to grin up at Eve. It was that doggy grin that did it, broke the patience Eve had been desperately clinging to.

"Mr. Maxwell, I would appreciate it if in the future you would keep that dog away from my front door. I've been standing out here fifteen minutes trying to get him to move and let me inside."

"I apologize. I was in the shower and forgot I'd let him out." He smiled that devil-may-care smile that turned the corners of his lips upward in wickedness and caused his dimples to appear.

Eve felt her anxiety climb as she noticed the tiny droplets of water that clung to his skin, as if reluctant to dry away. A knot began to pulsate in her lower jaw, and she clenched her hands in an effort not to reach out and touch him.

"Are you always so tense and uptight?"

"I beg your pardon?" Why was it that the man was always saying something to throw her completely off balance?

"Every time I see you, you seem stressed out. Your jaw is all knotted, and I'll bet your neck muscles are just screaming." Again that smile claimed his mouth. "I'm great at massages. A little baby oil and these hands, and you'd be completely relaxed."

"No, thank you, I like my screaming neck muscles just the way they are," she returned, stepping up to her front door.

"I've always found that making love is a good way to relieve tension."

For a moment Eve stared at him, unsure whether his statement was merely an idle comment or some kind of an invitation.

"And I'm sure you have no problems finding part-ners for that particular kind of stress management," she returned thinly.

"Actually, I'm rather picky about who I 'stress-relieve' with." His smile lost some of its wickedness. "I just think it would be nice if you weren't so up-tight."

"And I think it would be nice if you weren't so out-spoken." Eve bit her lip, stilling the rest of the things she would have liked to say to him. She wanted to tell him that it should be against the law to have a chest like his and bare it in public. She wanted to rail at him that it was a sin for his bedroom eyes to glitter with the promise of pleasures too exquisite to bear. But, of course, she didn't say any of these things. After all, she had to work for the man. She couldn't afford to alienate him completely. So instead she bit her tongue, nodded, and put her key in the lock of her front door.

"I just hope you don't turn into one of those old ladies . . ." His voice trailed off suggestively, and Eve paused and turned back to look at him.

"What old ladies?" she asked curiously.

"Oh, you know, one of those women who never smile and are so sour that nobody can live with them. They end up with blue hair and lots of cats."

For a moment, Eve could do nothing but sputter. Then, deciding not to dignify him with an answer, she shoved open her door. But as she started to go in, Fluffy ran out. The cat's sense of timing could not have been more appropriate.

Brice threw back his head and laughed. "My Lord, you're already halfway there."

Before Eve could return a suitably scathing reply, all hell broke loose. With a growl of excitement, Dog jumped off the porch after Fluffy. Brice yelled and ran after Dog, and Eve followed, certain that at any moment her sweet kitty would be torn to bits and devoured by Brice's vicious beast.

The chase went on for three blocks. Man after dog, dog after cat, and Eve struggling to keep up. She couldn't help but admire the easy grace Brice exhibited as he ran. Nor could she help but notice the way his tight jeans molded to his well-formed buttocks. Drat the man, anyway, she thought, huffing and puffing to catch up. Why couldn't he wear something in polyester? But even that thought didn't help. She had a feeling Brice Maxwell was the one man in the whole world who would manage to look sexy in polyester.

The chase ended abruptly as Fluffy found herself cornered against a chain-link fence. Dog barked ferociously, and Fluffy arched her back and hissed and spit.

Before Brice or Eve could intervene, Dog lunged forward, and Fluffy swung her paw, connecting with the dog's muzzle. Dog yelped in surprise, and blood immediately welled up on the end of his nose. Fluffy, with the cunning of instinct, used the dog's surprise to escape, leaping up and over the fence and disappearing beneath a large bush.

As Dog moved to stand next to Brice, pawing his bloody nose in bewilderment, Brice looked at Eve in surprise. "And you thought my dog was vicious! Your cat is a hellion!" he exclaimed.

"It was all your dog's fault," she returned, running a hand through her short hair in distraction.

"Do you want me to go see if I can find her?" Brice asked, gesturing toward the bush where Fluffy had fled.

Eve shook her head. "She'll come home later, when she knows your beast is securely locked up for the night."

They began the walk back to their duplex, a subdued Dog at their heels. "Whew," Brice breathed. "That was the first good run I've had since a month ago, when I had to run from a couple of students."

Eve looked at him curiously. "You ran from your students?"

"Only if they were angry with me and there were more than three of them."

"What kind of school did you work at?"

"A high school in Brooklyn," he answered, as if that explained everything.

"Why did you decide to come here?"

"I was ready for a change, a new challenge." His eyes no longer danced with amusement, but rather glittered with an intelligence Eve knew came not only from books, but from life, as well.

Yes, he looked like a man who would thrive on excitement, enjoy living on the edge. He looked like a man who would enjoy all the things she found frightening.

"I can't imagine what kind of a challenge you'll find here in Pawkinah, but I'm sure you will find it a change from New York City," Eve observed as they stepped up on their front porch.

Again those wicked points of light danced in his eyes. "Oh, believe me, I'm finding myself faced with a challenge that I'm anxious to pursue."

Eve felt a blush sweep over her, somehow knowing instinctively that he wasn't talking about his work. In fact, she had the distinct impression that he was talking about her. Well, he was in for a big surprise. The last thing she was going to do was fall into bed with a nefarious long-haired big-city man who'd probably be terminated from his job within a month.

"Good night, Mr. Maxwell," she murmured, and quickly disappeared into her home.

After she was gone, with the scent of her perfume still lingering around him, Brice sat down on the front porch, scratching absently behind Dog's half ear, his thoughts on his enticing neighbor.

Eve Winthrop... Yes, he saw her as a challenge. Her blushes enchanted him, encouraged him to say shocking things just to make the pink color creep up into her cheeks once again. It had been a long time since a woman had captured his interest, made him remember there were other things besides work.

There was something that drew him to Eve, a feeling that somewhere deep inside they were kindred souls. The problem was, Eve didn't appear to be in touch with her soul.

He'd seen her every day for the past three days, and he had yet to see her smile, hear her laugh. He wanted that. He wanted to see her sensual mouth stretched into a smile that was meant for him alone.

"What Eve Winthrop needs is an education in how to enjoy life," Brice murmured with a small smile. "And I think I'm just the man for the job." Dog whined and pawed at his blood-encrusted nose. "What do you think, Dog?" Brice asked, resuming scratching behind the dog's ear. "Do I have a chance with the lady? Or am I running the risk of having my nose bloodied?"

Dog had no answer.

Chapter Three

The early-morning air had a tangy nip to it as Eve left her house and headed down the sidewalk toward the school. It was only her first morning without her car, and already she regretted loaning it to Colleen. She'd had to get up a half hour earlier than usual in order to have time to walk to school.

She'd gone only about a half a block when she heard the throb of a motorcycle coming from behind her. She turned to see Brice pulling up alongside her on his monster machine. He flashed her a smile that gleamed as brightly as his silver-trimmed helmet. "Where's your car?"

"I loaned it to my sister for a couple of days," Eve answered, shouting to be heard above the throaty growl of the motorcycle.

"Hop on, I'll drive you to school." He gestured to the back seat and the helmet that hung from the sissy bar.

"No, thanks, I'll walk."

His eyes flashed with the fires of challenge. "What's the matter, Eve? Afraid?"

"Of course I'm not afraid." Despite the fact that she knew better, Eve couldn't help but rise to the challenge.

"Then ride with me." He smiled again, and Eve wondered if this was the same kind of grin the serpent had worn when he enticed the original Eve to eat of the forbidden fruit.

He reached behind him, grabbed the extra helmet and held it out to her. "Come on, Eve. Maybe you'll enjoy it."

Eve stared at the helmet as if it were some sort of horrible spider. She'd lied when she'd said she wasn't afraid. She'd never been on a motorcycle before, and the thought of riding on one terrified her. But it was much more than fear that made her hesitate. What if somebody saw her riding with him? What damage would be done to her reputation?

"It's only a couple of blocks," he coaxed, and despite her better judgment, almost with a will of their own, her hands reached out and took the helmet.

Before rational thought could talk her out of it, she jerked the helmet on, unsure what forces had her responding to his challenge.

She finished buckling the helmet strap beneath her chin, then eyed the small area of seat behind him. How was she ever going to sit on that small area and not touch him? It suddenly seemed vitally important that she have no physical contact with him. He was just too darned . . . male!

"Well?" He looked at her expectantly.

"Okay, okay . . ." she grumbled. She swung her leg up and over the bike, settling onto the seat gingerly. Instantly she realized there was a slight tilt to the leather-padded area that made it impossible to keep herself from sliding intimately against his backside. She held herself as stiff as possible, refusing to give in to the desire to mold herself to the warmth of his hard male body.

"Ready?" he asked, turning his head to flash her a smile of encouragement.

She nodded, too terrified to speak. What was she doing? She'd never been on a motorcycle before in her life. What if her students saw her? What if Mrs. Worthington saw her?

"You'd better hang on," he advised.

Hang on to what? she wondered. There were no convenient straps or handles to hold, there was nothing but Brice, and she wasn't about to grab hold of him. "I'm fine," she answered, giving him an Academy Award–winning smile of confidence.

As he started the machine and revved the engine, Eve's heart constricted with a thick fear. The throbbing engine pulsated through her, creating a strange hum that coursed through her body. When he put the bike in gear and it jumped forward, Eve swallowed a squeal as she nearly toppled backward off the bike. She grabbed for him, her arms snaking around his waist, her body stuck to his like a suction cup against a wet wall. She closed her eyes, deciding the only way to get through this particular experience was to treat it as a test of endurance, a mission of survival.

However, after the first block and a half, something began to happen. Eve opened her eyes, surprised to see how vivid the passing scenery looked without the confines of a car surrounding her.

Brice was traveling at a leisurely speed, and Eve was grateful for that. The breeze felt wonderful on her face, cool, invigorating and full of spring. But it was the scent of Brice that drifted back to her, enticed her. He smelled of hot summer nights, long-forgotten dreams. And freedom. Before she had time to assimilate where that particular thought had come from, she noticed other, more disturbing things.

His body was warm, his stomach flat and taut beneath her hands. She had a sudden image of colored bikini briefs and a tanned, firm stomach, taut buttocks, and well-formed shoulders. Heat swept through her, and at that moment Brice turned a corner. The motorcycle leaned, and Eve instinctively rode the curve, her legs tightening compulsively against his.

Despite her fear, in spite of her slight embarrassment at the intimate physical contact, she felt exhilarated, invigorated, more alive than she'd ever felt in her life.

She was almost disappointed when the ride ended and he pulled into the school parking lot and into his reserved space.

When he shut off the engine, Eve crawled off the bike, knowing her face flushed pink as she thought of the way her legs had pressed so tightly against his.

"Hi, Miss Winthrop."

Eve turned to see two of her female pupils. "Hello, Diane . . . Audrey." She groaned inwardly and greeted the girls with a nonchalance she didn't feel. She took off her helmet and handed it to Brice, who had also climbed off the machine.

"Hi, girls. I'll bet you didn't know Miss Winthrop was such a daring soul," Brice exclaimed.

The two girls looked shyly at Eve, then at Brice, and then scurried off, giggling behind cupped hands.

"Thanks a lot," Eve snapped. "I have enough problems gaining the respect of my students without you making them think I'm some kind of a motorcycle mama."

Brice laughed. "I prefer to think of you as my biker babe." He laughed again at her look of outrage. "Ease up, Eve. I probably just raised their respect level for you by at least twenty percent."

As they began to walk toward the school building, Brice grinned at her, his eyes the inviting shade of the sky. "Admit it—you enjoyed it."

She smiled. It was only a small one, as if she couldn't help it, but it was enough to make Brice's heart pound a little faster. He'd known a smile would do all kinds of wonderful things for her, and he'd been right. Even the small one that curved her lips held promise, made her green eyes sparkle brightly, gave her face a sensual animation. A ripple of anticipation stirred deep in his stomach as he imagined what she would look like with a full, generous grin on her face.

"It was different," she conceded, unwilling to admit to him that she had, indeed, enjoyed the ride. In truth, the blood was still pounding through her veins and adrenaline was pulsating inside her, making her feel as if she could handle anything life threw her way. But she didn't know whether this strange euphoria was a result of the ride on the motorcycle or due to the prolonged physical contact with Brice.

"I was wondering if you'd do me a favor," he said as they entered the school building.

"What kind of favor?" she asked hesitantly. She wanted as little to do with Brice Maxwell as possible. For some reason, when she was around him she felt as if she'd drunk one too many glasses of wine. She experienced a slight giddiness, a light-headedness that wasn't altogether unpleasant.

"I've planned to go over the student records today, assess what's working and what's not within the school structure. I'd like to make these assessments with the input of somebody who's worked within this system for some time. I wondered if you'd be willing to meet me in the office after school this afternoon.''

Eve's initial impulse was to give him a resounding no. She didn't want to place herself in a position where she had to spend any unnecessary time with him. Still, this was work-related, and it made her uncomfortable to think of Brice, who was not from this area, not familiar with their town, making decisions on school policy. It made her more than uncomfortable. It was a nightmare.

"Okay," she finally agreed. After all, what could possibly happen in his office in the afternoon?

As if he had read her mind, his eyes gleamed wickedly and he grinned that sexy smile that made Eve's knees weaken. "I promise I'll make it the most enjoyable trip to the principal's office you've ever experienced." With those words of promise, he turned and headed down the corridor.

By the time school finished for the day, Eve had decided she was courting danger by agreeing to help Brice. It didn't matter that he was the school principal, her boss. She'd been an absolute fool to agree to meet with him.

Earlier in the day, during the lunch period, she'd heard from several of the teachers that Brice was making the rounds of the classrooms, standing at the back and observing the teachers at work.

Eve's anxiety level immediately climbed as she anticipated his visiting her classroom. How could she make a good impression, dazzle him with her teaching skills, when all she could think about was the way his body heat had warmed her from the inside out as she'd ridden behind him on the motorcycle? How could she be professional when all she could think about was the way his stomach muscles had felt beneath her hands, the way his provocative scent had seemed to envelop her?

Now her footsteps echoed hollowly as she walked down the empty hallway toward the office. As usual, the teachers had all vacated the building before the sound of the students' departures had completely faded. Even the secretary's desk chair was empty when she entered the office.

She hesitated, gazing at the closed door that led to the principal's room. This is a mistake, she thought, smoothing her hands down the sides of her burgundy slacks. This is a mistake. She knew it with every fiber of her being. Except for old Joe, the sole member of the school's cleaning staff, who was probably sleeping down in the boiler room, she and Brice were alone in the building.

She shoved aside her misgivings and knocked on the door. *This is business,* she reminded herself firmly as his voice drifted through the door, bidding her enter.

She walked in, feeling, as always, a strange fluttering of her heart at the sight of him. He sat behind the antique oak desk, looking as fresh and vital as he had that morning. He rose as she came in, and the show of courtesy for some reason pleased her. At least the man isn't a total barbarian, she thought.

"I didn't realize it had gotten so late," he said, looking at his wristwatch in astonishment. "Please, have a seat." He resumed his place, shoving aside the paperwork in front of him.

Eve slid into the chair opposite the desk, feeling like a recalcitrant student about to receive a lecture.

"I've been going over records, figuring percentages, studying test scores, and I can't believe what I'm finding. This school is in appalling shape."

Eve blinked several times in surprise. "What do you mean?"

Once again he got up from the desk, his body almost vibrating with energy as he began to pace back and forth. "The dropout rate here in Pawkinah is comparable to an inner-city school in New York. The test scores are almost thirty percent lower than the national percentile." Brice seemed to consume the space and air around him, his virility and power evident in the tautness of his muscles, in his tense movements. "The football team hasn't won a season in over ten years. After-school activities—what few are offered—are only attended by a tenth of the student body. The teachers arrive with the pupils and leave at the same time. What happened to commitment? School pride?" He stared at her, then grinned suddenly, as if aware that he'd been ranting. "Sorry. I'm really not yelling at you. I'm merely yelling at the situation, and you happen to be an available scapegoat."

Eve smiled and nodded. "I believe I used you for the same purpose last night when I discovered your dog on my front porch." It was easy to smile. She was intensely relieved that the topic of conversation was indeed work.

Brice stopped his pacing, coming to stand next to the window, where the afternoon sunlight teased his hair, pulling a hint of auburn out of its dark depths. "I just don't understand how this has been allowed to happen . . . this complacency, not only among the students, but with the teachers, as well."

"You're using a pretty broad brush in painting everything black." Eve felt her feathers ruffling. After all, he was talking about her work, her colleagues. She couldn't help but be slightly offended by his words.

"I need a broad brush. This school has some major problems and needs a complete overhaul."

"It's amazing. How did we ever function before you arrived here?" Eve responded dryly, taking offense at his judgments.

"I can't imagine." He flashed her an arrogant, knowing grin. "I think there are several things around here that need my particular brand of renovation." His eyes glittered warmly, like the sparkling waters of a lake beckoning her to enter and enjoy.

"Perhaps there are some things better left alone," Eve countered uneasily.

"Hmm . . . I guess we'll just have to see." The blueness of his eyes changed, deepened, taking on a hint of challenge that both frightened and lured her.

"Anyway," he continued briskly, "I've got some ideas I'd like to bounce off you, see how you think the other teachers will respond to the proposed changes."

Eve nodded, relieved now that the conversation was back on business.

Brice sat down behind the desk again. "The first thing I intend to do is make it mandatory that the teachers arrive a half hour before the students in the mornings and stay an hour after school. They should be here for extra help, questions. Besides, how can we expect the students to be committed if the teaching staff isn't?"

Eve laughed. "That certainly won't win you any friends among the teachers."

"I'm not looking to make friends. I want to do what's best for the students."

Eve nodded thoughtfully. "Actually, it's a good idea. I'm afraid we've all gotten rather lazy since we've been functioning without a principal." Although Eve agreed with the extension of the hours, she knew several of the teachers would be quite unhappy. But he was right—an air of complacency did hang over the school.

"For my next idea, I need you to come with me." He stood up and moved to the door, looking at her expectantly.

"Where are we going?" Eve asked as she followed him out of the office and down the hallway.

"You'll see." He smiled at her enigmatically. "One of the most important things that needs to be accomplished is getting the students involved, giving them a reason to look forward to coming to school.''

''Easier said than done,'' Eve responded, hurrying to keep up with his long, confident strides.

''I've got an idea, something we did in New York.'' He stopped at the set of iron rungs that led up through the ceiling and to the roof of the building. ''A rooftop club.'' He grinned at her expectantly, his boyish enthusiasm making him look less threatening. ''Come on.'' He gestured for her to precede him up the steps.

She hesitated, unsure she wanted to be up on a roof with Brice. After all, she didn't know him at all. Maybe he was some kind of maniac.

He laughed at her hesitation. ''Eve, do you always think before you act? Don't you ever act on impulse?''

''Never,'' Eve returned decisively. ''Impulsiveness is for fools.''

''A little of it is good for the soul,'' Brice said with a grin.

''Then your soul must be quite healthy,'' Eve retorted sourly. She grabbed the rungs of the ladder and began to climb up, wondering why it was that Brice Maxwell evoked such volatile emotions in her.

Brice climbed up the ladder behind her, enjoying the view of her enticing behind just above him. He'd made her angry with his comment on impulsiveness. Her anger was obvious in the decisive wiggle of her bottom as she stomped up the stairs.

Oh, how she intrigued him, with her eyes of passion and her tight control. She reminded him of himself five years ago, burdened by too many responsibilities, shackled by self-imposed chains. What she needed was for somebody to help her break those bonds. The question was, was he the man for such a job?

As she reached the rooftop and turned to look at him, her eyes radiating a mixture of irritation and excitement, Brice knew he wanted to be the man who taught her how to enjoy living, enjoy loving.

He joined her on the flat roof, then walked with her over to the edge, where he leaned against the four-foot brick retaining wall. From the top of the three-story school, most of Main Street was visible. "What do people do around here for excitement on the weekends?" he asked, gazing out on the quiet little town.

Eve came to stand beside him. "There's the Bowl-O-Rama on the north side of town, the drive-in movie theatre to the south. Most of the kids hang out at the pizza place on Main. It's the only spot in town that has a jukebox. Then, of course, there's the Worthington Cemetery."

Brice turned and looked at her curiously. "Are the good people of Pawkinah into grave-robbing?"

"Not hardly. It's Pawkinah's version of a lovers' lane." She laughed, and Brice felt his breath catch in his chest. God, she was beautiful with the waning afternoon light dancing on her face and laughter kissing her lips. He felt a responsive curl of heat unfurl in his groin, spreading tendrils of flame through the pit of his stomach. Lovers' lane...oh, yes, he could imagine being with Eve in the confines of a car, her sweet scent surrounding him as he explored the curve of her neck, the texture of her skin, with his mouth. He could easily envision her graceful body splayed beneath his as the car windows fogged with their shared passion.

She must have seen the fire of desire clouding his eyes, for she took a step away from him and the laughter faded abruptly from her lips. "Did you bring me up here to discuss the social habits of the people of Pawkinah, or are you going to tell me your ideas for improving the school?"

"We could discuss your social habits." He grinned.

"I don't have time for social habits," she snapped. "And if you aren't going to talk business, then I really should be getting home." The look on her face told him she wasn't kidding. "Tell me about this rooftop club. What exactly is it?"

He smiled, defeated, although he certainly wasn't giving up for good. Sooner or later he was going to get beneath the defenses Eve had erected.

"Each week the students can earn points for good performance. After they've accumulated so many points, they get to come to the rooftop club for their lunch period. We'll provide pizza and soda for everyone." He paused a moment. "What do you think?" He looked at her expectantly.

"I think you're crazy," Eve blurted out. "Besides, from everything I've been reading lately, I understand that reward systems don't work well to motivate kids."

"This isn't part of a reward system," Brice told her. "It's a goal-oriented plan. It worked well in New York," he countered.

"Brice, this isn't New York City. Besides, Mrs. Worthington would never allow it. She'd never okay the funds to buy pizza and soda." Eve started back down the steps, Brice following her. When she reached the bottom, she looked at him once again. "I'm sorry, I just don't think the idea will fly. It's too... crazy." She started for the front door of the school, Brice hard on her heels.

"Mrs. Worthington knew what she was getting when she hired me. My past record attests to the fact that I don't always follow conventional methods."

"Seeing it on paper and living it in reality are two different things." Eve looked at her wristwatch. "I really should start home," she said.

"I'll drive you home. I'm ready to leave, too," Brice said when they reached the parking lot.

"No, I'd rather walk," Eve protested, more vehemently than she'd intended. She didn't want another ride on his motorcycle, didn't want the close physical contact with him again.

"Are you sure?" he asked, standing next to the monster machine. She nodded, and he continued, "I intend to go ahead with my rooftop club. If Mrs.

Worthington won't pay for it, then I'll pay out of my own pocket. We're competing with video games and MTV. We've got to give these kids something fun, a reason to want to come to school, or eventually we're going to lose them. I'm also planning a school dance."

Eve shook her head. "We haven't had a school dance in over five years. Mrs. Worthington doesn't believe in them."

"There's nothing in my contract that says I have to please Mrs. Worthington. She may own most of this town, but she doesn't own me." He moved closer to Eve, the flame of passion back in his eyes. "I'm my own man, Eve. Can you say that you're your own woman?"

She couldn't. In fact, she couldn't say anything. She had no breath—it had all been sucked away by his nearness. As he took another step toward her, his chest now touching hers, she knew she should step back. But her feet were frozen to the spot. She couldn't have moved at the moment if her life depended on it.

His eyes radiated the heat of a volcano, and she felt like a sacrificial virgin, knowing that if she jumped into the flames certain death would result, but unable to stop the inevitable plunge.

Before she had time to voice a desperate protest, his lips touched hers. Gently at first, like the whisper-soft feel of satin sheets against bare flesh, then deeper, harder, his tongue moving to explore the mysteries that lay within. His mouth tasted of white lightning and hot nights.

Eve couldn't help but respond to the sensual language of his lips. She answered him with her own, speaking in a language she didn't realize she knew.

He slowly withdrew his mouth from hers and smiled down at her. "Now that was an impulse."

Eve took a step backward, appalled at what she had just allowed to happen. "That was a mistake."

His smile widened as he reached for his helmet and put it on, covering up the dark length of his hair. "If that was a mistake, then you just compounded it."

"What do you mean?" she asked, still breathless from the tumultuous emotions racing through her.

He sat down on the bike and kick-started the motor. The motor roared to life, its throaty moan pulsating in the pit of her stomach. "I kissed you...but you kissed me back." With that, he winked at her and pulled away.

Eve stared after him, thinking of all that had just transpired. Rooftop clubs and dances...a lot of people were not going to be happy with the changes he intended to make at the school.

She reached up and gently touched her slightly swollen lips. But what really frightened her were the changes he threatened to make in her.

Chapter Four

"What's going on?" Eve muttered beneath her breath as she quickened her pace toward the school building. Even from half a block away she could see that something unusual was happening. A large crowd of students milled around on the front lawn of the school, their voices loud, full of excitement.

"What's going on here?" she asked, approaching the group of kids.

"Mr. Maxwell is up on the roof," one of the boys explained, his eyes sparking with excitement as he pointed a finger at the flat rooftop. "He says he'll stay up there every day that we have perfect attendance."

"Yeah, he's even put a tent up there to sleep in," another boy added, shaking his head and grinning crookedly. It was obvious he was quite impressed with

Brice, although Eve knew it would be considered un-cool for the boy to verbalize such admiration.

The kids probably thought Brice Maxwell was awe-some, but Eve could think of a few other choice adjectives to describe Brice—a nutcase, a Looney Tune, words to that effect.

She walked into the building and headed down the corridor toward her classroom. "The man is a total lunatic," she muttered as she moved into her room. "A raving fruitcake."

"People are going to start saying that about you if you don't stop talking to yourself," Margie exclaimed from her perch atop Eve's desk. "I guess you've heard the latest scoop—our esteemed principal and his roof sit-in?"

Eve nodded and dropped her stack of papers on the edge of her desk. "One of the students out front told me . . . something about attendance."

Margie's blond curls bounced with a rhythm all their own. "I guess our attendance yesterday was perfect, and that's what sparked this idea in our principal. He's well prepared. He's got a tent, some folding chairs and a sleeping bag up there."

"I wonder how prepared he is to talk to the school board members if they get wind of this little stunt," Eve returned, straightening a stack of books on a nearby shelf.

"Oh, they'll get wind of it, all right." Margie jumped down from the desk and smoothed a wrinkle out of her plaid skirt. "I heard that a couple of the students called the channel four newsroom."

Eve groaned. "Let's hope it's not a slow news day."

"When is it not a slow news day in Pawkinah?" Margie returned wryly. "Oh, well, I'd better head to class. With all the excitement around here, the kids are going to be monsters." With a wiggle of her fingers and a bounce of her curls, Margie disappeared out the door.

Roof sit-ins, news cameras... Brice Maxwell and his unorthodox methods were turning the school into a zoo. And Eve had a feeling the members of the school board would not be pleased.

It must have been a slow news day. Midmorning, a news crew arrived, complete with Minicams and a young female reporter. Lunch came and went. The teachers' lounge filled with talk of Brice. The general tone of the staff was one of bemusement. Members of the school board, notably Mrs. Worthington, were ominously absent from the day's activities.

It was after school when Eve decided to climb the stairs up to the roof and talk to Brice. She paused a moment at the bottom of the stairs to smooth her blue sweater, which topped navy slacks. A hand shot up to race through her short hair. She frowned, realizing she was primping. She stomped up the stairs, irritated with herself.

"Welcome to my humble abode," he said in greeting as she stepped onto the roof. He gestured to the small freestanding tent.

Eve approached him, shaking her head ruefully. "You have a talent for stirring things up, Mr. Maxwell."

"Ah, Miss Winthrop, trouble is worth it if the end result is something positive." He grinned at her. It was a charming, boyish grin that reflected a touch of rebellion. Even his clothes spoke of his desire to be unconventional. Tight, worn jeans, a pale blue cotton shirt, and an arrogance that suddenly reminded her of a movie she'd once seen.

"Just what this town needs, a clone of James Dean to cause a little excitement," she returned dryly.

Brice's grin widened. "But James Dean was a rebel without a cause. I'm a rebel *with* one."

"Brice, the only thing you're going to accomplish is to alienate the school board. They're a strong bunch, and they'll break you if you don't play the game their way." Eve bit her bottom lip in frustration.

He reached out and took her hand, leading her to where two folding chairs had been set up. He sat her down on one, then sat on the other one, pulling it up close enough that their knees touched. Eve tried to ignore the heat that instantly ignited when her kneecaps made contact with his.

"It doesn't matter how good the teaching staff is if there are no students to teach," he said, disconcerting her by not releasing her hand. His thumb began moving, creating tiny circles of sensation on the tender skin on the back of her hand. "If my little stunt gets the students coming to school every day, then it's worth a little static from the school board."

Eve nodded, seeing the method behind his madness. Besides, it was difficult to think coherently when he sat so close, when his outdoor scent surrounded her and his hand played havoc with her nerve endings.

She jumped up out of the chair, sweeping past him, needing some distance from his overwhelming presence. "I'm just worried that if you keep on this present course you may end up with a lot more than static."

He approached her with a smile. "I told you before, Mrs. Worthington had to know what to expect when she hired me. But I like it that you're worried about me. I didn't know you cared."

Eve flushed warmly. "Don't be ridiculous," she told him. "I just don't want to see us without a principal once again." Her face warmed even more when he flashed her another brilliant smile.

The man should be arrested for carrying a concealed weapon, she thought, his smile making her as weak-kneed, as dizzy, as a blow to the head. She looked at her wristwatch, trying to regain her equilibrium. "Well, I guess I'd better go home."

"Before you go, I have a couple favors to ask you." Brice managed to look sheepish. "I planned this little challenge to the students rather suddenly this morning. I had the tent and the sleeping bag from my camping-out days. But there are a few things I didn't consider, such as the care of Dog, and supper for myself." He dug into the pocket of his jeans and pulled out a key. "Would you mind feeding Dog while I'm up here?"

She hesitated, looking at the key he held. She wanted to say no. She didn't want to get any more involved with this man. And she particularly didn't want to have anything to do with his mangy mutt.

"I'd really appreciate it, Eve. Dog and I don't know anyone else to ask."

"Okay," she agreed reluctantly, taking the key from him. After all, she couldn't very well let the poor pooch starve, and it seemed reasonable that he should ask her, since she lived right next door.

"And would it be too much to ask if you'd bring me something to eat later this evening? I'd be glad to pay you for your trouble."

"You don't have to pay me," Eve returned. "Consider it my show of school spirit." She looked at him curiously. "Are you really going to stay up here all night?"

He nodded. "And every night that we have perfect attendance. It's a matter of honor. I've told the kids I will, so now I have to follow through."

"What if it rains?"

"Then I might get wet," he returned easily. "I've got my tent. I should be just fine."

Eve nodded and walked over to the ladder that led down. "I'll be back later this evening."

She breathed a sigh of relief as she left the roof. There was something about Brice that sucked her energy, overwhelmed her senses. He was more alive than anyone else she'd ever known. His very aliveness showed how dull, how empty, her own life was.

As she walked home, she made a mental note to call Colleen and find out when she could get her car back. If she was going to be running back and forth to school twice a day, she really needed an automobile.

She let herself into her duplex and was greeted by Fluffy's plaintive meow. "Hello, kitty." She reached down and gave the cat a quick pat on the back, then walked into the kitchen where she dropped her pile of books and papers on the table.

It was her habit to grade papers and work on the next day's assignment right after school. However, at the moment, the idea sounded boring. Her head was still too filled with Brice's vitality for her to settle down to grading papers. Besides, his house key was burning a hole in her pocket, urging her to forget her normal routine and instead rush right over there to see where he lived, see if she could glean something more about the man from his intimate surroundings.

Strange, how he excited such curiosity in her, such interest. She couldn't deny it anymore. Although he was nothing like what she'd once imagined she wanted in a man, there was something about him that excited her.

She left her place and went across the porch, unlocking the door cautiously, worried about Dog's reaction to her intrusion. She needn't have worried. As she stepped through the front door, Dog greeted her, his tail wagging so spasmodically that it moved his entire back end. He scratched at the door, then turned and looked at her, his brown eyes full of silent appeal. She opened the door once again, and the animal ran outside. Eve hoped he was smart enough to come back when he finished his business.

She turned her attention to the interior of the duplex. The setup of the rooms was just like her place, though the floor plan was exactly opposite.

She stood in the living room, although in this case it was difficult to think of it as a room for living. It was sparsely furnished, with a television set, a large gray corduroy recliner and a stereo unit. There were no records scattered about, no pictures on the walls, no knickknacks sitting around. There was a transitory air to the place, as if everything could be easily whisked into a moving van on a whim.

Yet she knew Brice wasn't an aimless drifter moving from place to place with the direction of the wind. She'd heard through the grapevine that he'd been a principal at his last school for six years. That certainly wasn't the record of a drifter.

She walked into the kitchen, unsurprised to see the rooms looking sterile and unused. A coffeemaker and an electric can opener were the only evidence of occupancy. Hadn't she read someplace that you could tell a lot about people by the contents of their refrigerators? She opened the fridge door and stared. A half-full bottle of ketchup, a gallon of milk, and a jar of dill pickles. If the unusual collection of foodstuffs knew anything about Brice Maxwell, they weren't talking.

She moved on to the bedroom, where there was a double bed and a chest of drawers. The bed was made up with black-and-white sheets with a bold geometric pattern. They were slightly rumpled, one of the pillows still holding the indentation of his head. Without any conscious will on her part, she walked across the room and touched the bed with the palm of her hand, wondering if his body heat would still be there.

She snatched her hand back when a loud scratching sounded at the front door. Remembering Dog, and cursing her own foolishness, she left the bedroom and hurried to let the dog back in.

Dog ran in, heading directly toward the kitchen and the pet dish on the floor. He skidded to a halt before the empty dish, then turned and looked at her expectantly.

"All right, just a minute," Eve muttered, opening cabinets in search of dog food. "Ah, here we go," she said, spying a large bag of dry food beneath the sink. Using the scoop from the bag, she quickly filled the dish. Checking to make sure he had plenty of water, she gave him a tentative pat on the head. He really was the ugliest mutt she'd ever seen.

Leaving Dog happily enjoying his supper, she moved out of the kitchen. She paused at the front door, her gaze once again sweeping the living room. The transitory air of the place seemed to embody the spirit of the man who lived here. Restless, impetuous, impulsive... Free. She frowned. Strange, how that last adjective had jumped into her head. "Free indeed." She relocked his door and pulled it closed behind her. "Free to make a fool of himself," she muttered, crossing the porch to her side of the duplex.

Walking into her kitchen, she picked up the telephone receiver, intent on calling Colleen and getting her car back. If her sister was home, she wasn't answering, because her answering machine clicked on.

"Colleen, this is Eve. I need my car back this evening. If I'm not here when you come by, then I'll be at the school...up on the roof." She smiled as she replaced the receiver, thinking of Colleen's curiosity when she heard the message. The odds were good that Colleen would show up at the school later in the evening, if for no other reason than to see what Eve was doing.

That issue taken care of, Eve sat down at the kitchen table and began grading students papers.

It was nearly six o'clock when she finished the last of her work and stretched, trying to obtain her second wind. She went into the bedroom and quickly changed clothes, pulling on a pair of jeans and a pale pink sweatshirt. Her stomach gurgled with pangs of hunger, reminding her that Brice was probably hungry, as well.

She certainly couldn't drive through a hamburger stand, not without her car, but she had plenty of food to provide a picnic of sorts.

As she packed a basket, she decided that she would eat with him. He'd probably welcome the company. Being up on the roof for any length of time had to get lonely. She scoffed inwardly at the thought. Brice Maxwell seemed too self-possessed ever to feel the ache of loneliness.

The sun had faded to the muted gold of pretwilight as she made her way back to the school. The air was warm, whispering that the blistering heat of summer was just around the corner. She wondered if Brice would be around to enjoy a Pawkinah summer. He'd been contracted for the remainder of this year and all of next year. But Eve knew that if he didn't please Irene Worthington, then the older woman would find a way to terminate the contract. She'd done it in the past, and she certainly wouldn't hesitate to do it again.

But that's not my concern, Eve reminded herself. Brice's future, or lack of one, in Pawkinah had nothing to do with her. All he was to her was her boss, and her neighbor, and that was all she intended their relationship to be.

Still, it was difficult to rationalize why her heart thudded erratically when she climbed to the top of the stairs and saw him. He sat on the sleeping bag, which was spread out beneath him. His legs were crossed, Indian-style, and his head bent over as he read a book that lay open in his lap.

As she stepped onto the roof, he looked up, and those intense blue eyes mirrored the smile that curved his lips. Her heart leapt into her throat, and she felt a wave of warmth creep up her neck and across her face.

She had heard of bedroom eyes, but Brice had a bedroom face. When he smiled like that, a strange warmth invaded her limbs, making her feel as if she were on the verge of illness. She suddenly remembered the brief kiss they had shared, and she wondered what it would feel like to have her lips claimed by his in a kiss of flared passion.

She shook her head, dispelling the mental projections. "Are you hungry?" she asked briskly as he rose and moved toward her.

"Starving," he answered, his gaze lingering on her mouth, making her think he was not talking about food.

She fought the impulse to wet her mouth, finding it suddenly incredibly dry. "Great, I've got chicken." She shoved the basket into his hands, her blush growing warmer as his grin deepened.

"There's nothing better than a luscious thigh or a plump breast." His voice was blatantly suggestive as he grinned at her.

"You are incorrigible," Eve returned.

He merely laughed. It was full-bodied expression of joy that made her toes curl up inside her shoes. "Come, sit down." He knelt down on the sleeping bag and patted the area next to him. When she joined him, he opened the basket and peered inside. "You've got enough food in here to feed five people," he exclaimed, taking out the foil-wrapped fried chicken, along with containers of potato salad and baked beans. "You're joining me, right?"

She nodded, helping him unpack the remainder of the food.

"When on earth did you have time to do all this?" he asked as they began filling their plates.

"I did most of it yesterday," she explained. "I usually spend Sunday afternoons cooking things for the upcoming week."

"Ah, my organized, well-planned Eve." He reached out and lightly touched the end of her nose, then turned his attention to the plump chicken leg on his plate.

Eve stared down at her own plate, her nose burning where he'd made contact. *My Eve.* The possessive sound of the words shot a thrill right through her.

For the next few minutes, they sat in a comfortable silence, enjoying the food and the night clouds that were creeping in to claim the last lingering glow of twilight. As the darkness deepened, Brice pulled a lantern out of the tent and lit it, creating an intimate pool of golden illumination around them.

She studied him surreptitiously while they ate. He fascinated her, from the top of his shining dark hair to the soles of his feet. From the thick lashes of his blue eyes to the sensual curve of his lips. Never had a man intrigued her like this one, and never had she felt less sure of her own ability to maintain a safe distance.

A car drove by on the street below, the horn honking and kids yelling out the window. Brice walked over to the edge of the building and waved down to the kids. "I'm sure they're checking up on me to make sure I'm still up here," he said, sitting down next to her again, his body heat warming her from the inside out.

"I fed Dog," she said inanely, needing conversation to ward off dangerous thoughts.

"Thanks. I was worried about him."

"He's the ugliest dog I think I've ever seen in my life," she observed.

Brice grinned and nodded. "Yea, he gives new meaning to the term *dog-ugly*. But he's loyal and smart, and at the time he came into my life we needed each other."

"What do you mean?" she asked, setting her now-empty plate aside.

"I was having a sort of gray day, sitting in a little neighborhood park feeling sorry for myself. Dog came prancing up and sat down beside me." Brice smiled. It was a small smile that spoke of pleasant memories. "He looked like hell. It was obvious he'd just been in a hell of a fight. His ear was bloody and torn nearly off, and he had cuts and welts all over. I looked at him and thought, 'Now, this guy's got it bad. At least I'm not bleeding and I've got both ears." He set his plate aside. "When I left the park, Dog followed me home, and he's been with me ever since."

"What was giving you a gray day?" Eve asked, and was immediately sorry. She didn't want to know anything personal about him. To know might be to care, and with all her family demands, she didn't have the time or the energy for anyone else in her life.

"My work," he answered, making her sigh in relief. That didn't sound so personal.

"What about your work?"

Gone was the arrogance, the devil-may-care expression that always gave his face such animation. Instead, his eyes darkened and his brow wrinkled in thought. "Working at an inner-city school in New York City is an experience every teacher, every principal, should have at least one time or another. It makes you appreciate any school you work at thereafter."

"Did you pull a lot of stunts like this back in New York?"

He nodded. "I turned myself inside out trying to light a flame, motivate the kids to want to learn. Unfortunately, they had more important things to contend with . . . like surviving."

"What do you mean?" She edged closer to him, drawn to the intensity that tensed his face.

In one fluid movement, he stood up and walked over to the edge of the roof, staring blankly at the streets below. He waved again, apparently to more kids driving by to make sure he was honoring his challenge.

The keen emotion on his face had not diminished when he continued speaking. "The kids at the school were better armed than the cops out on the streets. Drugs and gangs were rampant. I tried everything I could think of to try to turn things around. Oh, I had some successes, students I managed to touch, but it was like trying to catch raindrops in a sieve. So many escaped. I wanted to make a difference, but after six years of trying I realized the problem was too big for me to fix."

Eve saw the frustration that tensed his shoulders. She got up and walked over to him, placing a hand gently on his arm. "You can make a difference here, Brice. Pawkinah needs somebody like you."

"What about you, Eve? Do you need somebody like me?"

Before she had a chance to respond, he whirled around. He took her by the shoulders, and his eyes were blue fire when he pressed his lips to hers.

She had no chance to prepare herself, no time to mount defenses against the immediate assault on her senses. Vague warning signals flashed and blinked in the back of her brain, but they were quickly swallowed up in the intensity of the kiss.

His mouth burned hers, his tongue reaching inside to taste more fully. His arms gathered her close, molding her body intimately to his own.

With a groan of acquiescence, Eve moved her arms to embrace him, finding the length of his dark hair wonderfully erotic as she tangled her hands in it.

"Ah, Eve," he whispered, pulling his lips from hers and moving them down the length of her neck. She dropped her head back, allowing him easier access to the curve of her jawline, the base of her throat.

She was lost...lost in the scent of him, the touch of him, the feel of his body warm against her own. He was manna for her soul, the very breath of life, and she clung to him, wanting everything he offered.

"Yoo-hoo! Eve, are you up there?" Colleen's voice drifted up from the bottom of the ladder. The voice blasted Eve from her haze of sensuality, right back to the sanity of reality.

Chapter Five

Eve jumped away from Brice as if he were the devil himself and it was the fires of hell that burned in her veins. She stared at him, horrified by the momentary lapse into passion's insanity.

"Eve...are you up there?" Colleen's voice called out once again.

Eve hurried to the stairs and answered. "I'm here. Come on up." She turned to Brice. "It's my sister," she explained. By the glow of the lantern she could see amusement glittering in the dark depths of his eyes. It was an amusement that sparked an answering edge of anger in her.

Did he think this was some kind of game? Was this the kind of challenge he'd spoken about the other night—bedding down one of his teachers?

She flushed and ran a hand through her short dark hair in distraction, knowing she was probably over-reacting to the whole situation. After all, they'd only shared a simple kiss. She reached up and touched her lips. They felt swollen and red. There had been nothing simple about his kiss.

"What in blazes are you doing up here?" Colleen exclaimed as she stepped onto the roof, looking first at Brice, then at Eve. She shook her blond-streaked hair, her eyes flashing with curiosity. "I couldn't believe it when I listened to my answering machine and it said you'd be up on the roof of the school. What on earth is going on?"

"Nothing is going on," Eve said quickly. "Mr. Maxwell is taking part in a challenge to the students, and I merely did him a favor by bringing him some supper."

"Yes, we heard about Mr. Maxwell's student challenge," Colleen replied thinly.

Brice's dark eyebrows shot up quizzically. "We?"

"Mrs. Worthington and I," Colleen returned. She looked back at Eve. "I have your car here, but I was hoping I could keep it for another couple of days."

Eve frowned. "Colleen, I really need it back."

"Yes, but I need it," Eve's younger sister protested.

Flashing Brice a look of apology, Eve took Colleen by the arm and pulled her over to the edge of the roof. "Haven't you gotten your car retagged yet? I gave you the money to take care of it. I thought you were going to do it this morning.''

"I know, I know, but I had to use the money for something else. Can't I keep the car for another few days?'' Colleen's voice took on the whining quality that always made Eve's teeth ache. "I can't function without a car, and I don't have the money to do mine.''

Eve sighed. "If I loan you some more money, will you use it to take care of your tags?'' she whispered, embarrassed to be having this conversation in front of Brice. Still, to his credit, he'd busied himself cleaning up the remains of their dinner.

"I suppose if you lend me the money I could do it in the morning, although you know how much I hate dealing with those people down at Motor Vehicle.'' Spoiled petulance pursed Colleen's bottom lip.

Eve ignored it and instead held out her hand. "My keys?''

With a sigh of exasperation, Colleen dropped the car keys into Eve's hand.

"I'll take you home,'' Eve said.

Colleen nodded, and the two of them walked back over to where Brice was packing the last of the left-overs back into the basket.

Eve smiled her thanks and took the basket from him. "I guess I'd better go. I'm taking Colleen home.''

"Thanks for supper,'' he said, his eyes searching her face as if he were seeking out secrets. He reached out his hand as if to stroke her cheek, then let it fall to his side, his gaze shooting from Eve to Colleen and back again. "Everything all right?"

"Eve . . . let's go," Colleen exclaimed impatiently.

Eve smiled distractedly at Brice. "I'll see you tomorrow." With a small wave, she walked over to Colleen, and together the two sisters left the roof and headed for the car.

"I certainly hope you aren't getting personally involved with that man," Colleen said as they pulled out of the school parking lot.

"Why?" Eve wondered why Colleen would say such a thing. She'd certainly never expressed any interest in Eve's personal relationships before.

"There's something about that man I don't like. Besides, Mr. Brice Maxwell probably won't be around here for too long. Mrs. Worthington is not particularly pleased with him. He's not what she expected."

"She had his résumé before she hired him, she checked out his references. Surely she knew what to expect," Eve protested, surprised to find herself defending Brice.

"Mrs. Worthington thought a lot of his craziness was because he was working in a large inner-city school. She didn't expect him to bring that same craziness here to Pawkinah." Heavy scorn colored Colleen's voice.

"It's not craziness," Eve told her. "He's just committed to finding a way to reach the kids."

"He'd better find a way to reach Mrs. Worthington, or he'll be out of here," Colleen returned.

Eve pulled up in front of Colleen's apartment building.

"All I know," Colleen continued, "is that you'd be ten kinds of crazy to get involved with a man like that."

"Why do you keep saying that?" Eve threw the car into park and turned to look at her sister. "There is certainly nothing going on between Mr. Maxwell and myself."

"Then why are you taking him supper?"

"Because he's my neighbor and he's my boss and he asked me to," Eve explained patiently.

"Harrumph," Colleen snorted in disbelief.

"What does that mean?"

Colleen's green gaze danced across Eve's face in speculation. "All I know is when I stepped on that roof, there was a tension between you that was thick. It was like I'd interrupted a big fight—or the two of you making out."

"Colleen!" Eve felt her face flush hotly... guiltily. "Your imagination is getting away from you." Her gaze skittered away from her younger sister.

"All I'm saying is that you'd be completely nuts to get involved with him. He'd break your heart." She opened her car door and stepped out. "Oh, by the way—" she leaned down to look in at Eve "—Mom has a clogged drain and wondered if you could stop by tomorrow night and fix it."

Eve nodded. "I'll take care of it."

"Also, Eddie is taking me out to some fancy place for dinner next Friday night. Can I borrow your blue dress to wear?"

"Come by one night this week and get it," Eve told her. Saying goodbye, she watched until her sister disappeared into the apartment building. Then she pulled away and headed for her house.

Ten kinds of crazy . . . Eve thought of Colleen's words as she took Brice his supper the next evening.

Yes, she would have to be crazy to get involved with a man like Brice. Besides the fact that, according to Colleen, he wouldn't be around for long, there was also the fact that they were very different from one another—too different.

With that thought in mind, she climbed the stairs to the roof, her heart steeled against the pleasure the sight of him always evoked.

"You're earlier today," he observed, taking the sack she offered him. "What culinary delights have you brought for me today?"

"Meat-loaf sandwiches, potato chips, and a hunk of chocolate cake," Eve answered, wondering why all of a sudden all she could think of was the kiss they had shared the night before. His lips had been so warm and soft. Where would the kiss have led if Colleen hadn't appeared with her timely interruption? The thought was provocative . . . scary.

"I can't stay," she said, hoping her voice didn't sound as strangled as she suddenly felt. "I'm on my way over to my mom's house. She has a clogged drain that needs to be fixed.''

Brice looked at her thoughtfully. It was the same expression he'd worn for a moment the night before, as if he were trying to see all the secrets of her soul. ''The family plumber, the local car loaner, money-lender... Has your family always taken advantage of you?''

''What?'' Eve stared at him incredulously.

''You heard me,'' he returned, taking her hand and pulling her to sit down beside him on the sleeping bag.

''My family doesn't take advantage of me,'' she protested. ''Well, maybe they do a little bit... but I don't mind.... I mean, I don't mind too much....'' She broke off, frustrated at her inability to sort out the family dynamics. She took a deep breath and began again. ''When my father died several years ago, Mom and Colleen sort of fell apart. It seemed natural that they lean on me a little more heavily.''

''From what I saw last night with your sister, they lean much too heavily on you.''

Eve waved her hand in irritation. ''What do you know about family and responsibilities? Most people in Pawkinah believe you were hatched.''

Brice threw back his head and laughed, unsurprised to learn what the townspeople thought of him. In truth, it was going to take him a while to get used to the slower pace, the gossip, the small-town mentality of Pawkinah.

He sobered, looking at Eve, noting how the soft evening light dusted her face in golden hues. Did she have any idea how beautiful she was? He thought not. There was an unselfconsciousness about her, a lack of self-awareness that was attractive.

But what worried him now was the concern he felt for her as he remembered the scene he'd witnessed between her and Colleen. That, coupled with the tidbits of gossip he'd heard concerning Eve and her family, had evoked memories of his own past.

"Eve." He reached out and took her hand in his, enjoying the way it fit into his larger one. "Contrary to popular belief, I do have a family. My mother and father are wonderful, giving people. So giving, in fact, that it very nearly destroyed us all."

"What do you mean?" she asked, withdrawing her hand from his, finding it difficult to concentrate on what he was saying when his hand was so warm and inviting around hers. Besides, his words intrigued her.

He hesitated a long moment, his eyes distant, as if he were reaching for a nearly lost memory. "I was a late baby. My mother was almost forty, and my dad was fifty. They had tried for years to have children, and when I finally came along they were completely besotted with me. They loved me to distraction." He smiled. It was a soft one, not meant for her, but rather a reflection of his feelings for his parents. The smile slowly faded. "I was spoiled rotten, and I quickly learned that if I made a mistake my parents would do everything in their power to clean it up."

He stood up, his head filled with memories of the boy he had once been. They were not pleasant memories. "The more mistakes I made, the harder my parents worked to keep me out of trouble. As I got older, my messes got bigger." He sighed. "Oh, in the grand scheme of things, my messes were pretty harmless. Skipping school, smoking in the bathroom, speeding tickets, running with a group of kids who weren't exactly good students. Sound familiar?"

Eve nodded reluctantly, immediately thinking of Colleen. In the past three years, Eve had expended a lot of energy cleaning up Colleen's messes. They hadn't been monumental problems, just small irritations that Colleen refused to take responsibility for.

"Anyway, when I was a senior in high school, things culminated, and I found myself arrested and thrown into jail."

Eve gasped. "For what?"

Brice smiled. "A bunch of us decided we didn't like the color of a statue in a nearby neighborhood park, so we spray-painted it hot pink. We were caught red-handed—or, in this case, pink-handed."

"Brice, you don't have to tell me all this." She got up and went over to where he stood. "You were a kid, you made mistakes. We all make mistakes when we're young."

He shook his head. "Please, let me finish. I think it's important that you hear this." He continued. "I sat in jail, waiting for my parents to come and bail me out, smooth things over. After all, they'd always done so in the past. Only this time they didn't come. I waited and waited, but they didn't show up."

"What did you do?"

"At first I was angry. I couldn't figure out why they weren't there to clean up this mess." For just a moment, his eyes reflected his past inner turmoil, and Eve caught a glimpse of the boy he'd once been. The fire of rebellion burned in his eyes, a youthful rebellion not tempered by maturity or wisdom. Then he straightened his shoulders, and Eve saw the man he had become. The rebellion was still there, but it was different now, mingled with respect and a focus.

"The anger gave way to fear, and finally acceptance. I stayed in jail for three days, and during that time I did a lot of thinking. Mom and Dad had made it easy for me to mess up, but ultimately I had to accept responsibility for myself and my own actions." He walked back over to the sleeping bag and sat back down, waiting for her to rejoin him before he continued.

"When my parents finally came for me, I looked at them, really looked at them for the first time. I realized how tired they were, how much of themselves they had used up on me. From that moment on, my life changed. I learned to accept the consequences of my actions, I gained my self-respect. I learned that I didn't need to depend on anyone but myself, and my parents got back their life."

"Brice, I don't see what this—"

He interrupted her by placing his hands on the tops of her shoulders. He smiled softly at her. It made her toes tingle and a warmth spread throughout her body. "You're doing the same thing to Colleen that my parents did to me. You're encouraging her to be irresponsible."

She pulled away from him, slightly irritated by what he was saying. Colleen's irresponsibility wasn't her fault. What made Brice Maxwell think he knew what was going on with her family?

"Oh, Eve, I see so much life in you, such promise." He reached up and, with one hand, gently stroked the side of her face. "I don't want you to be like my parents and wake up one morning and find that life has passed you by, that you gave everything you had to everyone else and have nothing left for yourself."

It was difficult to maintain her anger when his ultimate concern was for her. As his fingers moved across her lips, stroking the fullness of the lower one, she fought the impulse to capture his finger with her mouth. "It sounds to me like your mother and your sister could use a shot of self-respect and you could use a life of your own. Take a chance, Eve, start living for yourself—now, before they use you up. It's the best thing you can do for yourself, and the kindest thing you can do for them."

She knew he was going to kiss her. The intent was in his eyes before his lips began to descend. She jumped up, away from him. She needed time to think, time to assess what he'd said, and one thing she couldn't do while he kissed her was think.

"It—it's getting late. My mother will be waiting for me." She grabbed her purse and headed for the stairs.

"Eve?"

She paused and turned back to look at him.

"You could always turn over a new leaf right here and now. Call your mother and tell her to get a plumber, then come back here and really start living." His eyes glittered with the wickedness that she now realized was as much a part of him as his dark hair and his startling blue eyes. "Have you ever made love in a tent on top of the roof of a school building?" His smile held blatant invitation.

"You, Mr. Maxwell, are a very naughty man." With those words, Eve went down the stairs, and Brice's answering laughter warmed her heart all the way to her car.

On the way to her mother's house, Eve thought about Brice. He excited her, he confused her . . . but, more than anything, he frightened her.

He offered her things she was afraid to accept. His eyes held an intensity, a passion, that she knew would change her forever if she was foolish enough to imbibe. Change frightened her. Like Brice, change was unpredictable.

She parked her car in her mother's driveway, noticing that the grass needed mowing and the flower beds were crying out for tending. She always dreaded having these chores added to her already busy schedule.

With a small sigh, she grabbed the bottle of liquid drain cleaner she'd bought and headed for the front door.

"Oh, Eve, honey, I thought you'd never get here." Her mother greeted her with a kiss on the cheek. "I just don't know what's the matter with that kitchen drain. It's just not working properly." She led Eve into the kitchen and over to the sink, where a tub of brackish water waited.

After reading the instructions on the side of the bottle, Eve poured the contents into the standing water. "Now, we need to let it work for thirty minutes, then flush it out with hot water. How about a cup of tea while we wait?"

"Oh, yes, that would be lovely." Violet sat down at the table while Eve filled the teakettle and placed it on the stove.

"Have you talked to Colleen today?" Eve asked as she got out the cups and tea bags. "I was wondering if she got her car taken care of."

"She did. She called me on her lunch hour." Violet smiled. "She sure does like her job with Mrs. Worthington."

"I just hope it lasts longer than her previous jobs," Eve returned, getting the milk and sugar and setting them on the table.

"Now, Evie, I'll admit Colleen has had a few problems settling into a job she likes." Violet smiled indulgently. "But Colleen has always been something of a free spirit."

"Mom, there's a difference between being a free spirit and being a flake," Eve retorted dryly.

"Eve, don't be so hard on your sister," Violet admonished, saying exactly what Eve had expected her to. It was an old conversation, one that was repeated over and over again, with very few variations.

The teakettle whistled shrilly, and Eve swallowed a sigh. She poured their tea and joined her mom at the table.

"This is the time of year your dad was always working in the backyard." Violet stared out the kitchen window, her pale blue eyes misting. "That man loved his flower beds. If only he was still here."

Eve reached across the table and captured her mother's soft, wrinkled hand with her own. "Mom, Dad has been gone for three years. He's not coming back, and you need to get on with your life."

"I just get so lonely. I rattle around alone in this big old house." She looked at Eve. "I don't see why you couldn't move back in here. Then I wouldn't be so lonely, and you'd be right here when I need you."

Eve fought down the impulse to agree just to please her mother. On an emotional level, she wanted to make things as easy as possible for her mother. But, remembering the conversation she'd just had with Brice, she recognized that moving in with her mother would be the worse possible thing for both of them. "Mom, maybe an alternative would be to sell this house and move into an apartment."

"Oh, goodness, your father would roll over in his grave if I sold this place." Violet looked horrified at the very thought.

"Mom, Daddy would want you to be happy," Eve countered gently. "This big house is too much for you. At the Hacienda apartments there are a lot of retired people. I've heard they have all kinds of social gatherings and even take trips together. You could make some new friends."

"Oh, posh, I don't need new friends. I've got you, and that's all I need." Violet smiled at her daughter and sipped her tea.

Eve smiled back, fighting off the feeling that she'd been plunged underwater and was slowly drowning.

It wasn't until much later, when she was on her way home, that she reviewed her conversation with her mother in her head. It was strange—since talking to Brice, she'd noticed things about her relationship with her mother and her sister that she'd never really noticed before. Brice's telling her about his life had given her a curious new insight into her own. It was at that moment that she decided that perhaps Brice was right. Now all she had to do was decide what she was going to do about it.

Chapter Six

All the next day, Eve thought about her family, alternating between liking the comfort and security of the status quo and knowing that Colleen and her mother were slowly draining her dry.

Now that she thought about it, the one halfway serious relationship she'd had—with Dwayne Hilton, the PE teacher at school—hadn't worked out because Dwayne had tired of playing second fiddle to the demands of her family. When Dwayne had given her an ultimatum—him or her family—the choice had been easy. She'd told Dwayne goodbye.

But now Eve realized she wanted more out of life than what her mother and her sister could offer her. There was an emptiness, a loneliness, that struck her at odd times of the day and night. There were times when she wished she was making coffee for two, when she longed to share her closet space with a male partner whose clothes would hang intimately next to hers. There were nights when she ached with an unfulfillment she couldn't quite name.

"What are you looking so glum about?" Margie asked at lunchtime, dropping her lunch tray on the table next to Eve's.

"Not glum, I'm just thinking," Eve returned, scooting over to give Margie space next to her on the bench.

"Thinking about what?" Margie asked, carefully picking the carrots out of her chef's salad.

"Family."

"Oh, no wonder you look glum," Margie replied, starting to separate the celery pieces from the rest of the salad.

Eve watched her for a moment. It was a daily ritual. Margie always bought a chef's salad, then proceeded to pick it all apart. "Margie...your father passed away several years ago, right?" Margie nodded, and Eve continued. "Is your mom real dependent on you?"

Margie laughed. "My mom doesn't slow down long enough to be dependent on anyone. She's got her bridge club and her volunteer work. She stays twice as busy as I do." Eve sighed, and Margie looked at her speculatively. "Is your mom making you crazy?"

"Not crazy—at least, not exactly. It's just that since Dad's death she's closed herself off to everyone but me. She doesn't go out of the house, she has no friends. She says I'm all she needs."

Margie whistled softly beneath her breath. "That sounds ominous."

"Don't get me wrong," Eve said hurriedly. "I love my mom and Colleen, and I like the fact that the three of us are close, but I'm beginning to wonder if maybe it isn't possible to be too close."

"So what are you going to do about it?"

Eve shrugged. "That's what's been on my mind all day. I guess I'm going to make some changes."

"Speaking of changes . . . have you heard about the memos that came from Mr. Maxwell this morning? Everyone got a copy in their mailbox."

Eve shook her head. "I haven't gone into the office to get my mail yet."

"Mr. Maxwell wants us to prepare lesson plans a week in advance instead of just daily, and he's setting up mandatory weekly meetings to discuss problems and goals." Margie paused a moment to chew a bite of salad, then continued in a lower voice. "I've heard a lot of grumbling about the extra work and time from some of the other teachers."

Eve smiled. "We've always had grumblers in this building."

"Yes, but these grumblers are some of Mrs. Worthington's minions." Margie grinned. "But I have a feeling Brice Maxwell can take care of himself, don't you?" Her grin widened. "Which reminds me, you never did tell me what the deal was with you and Mr. Maxwell exchanging clothing.''

"And I don't intend to tell you now." Eve laughed at Margie's crestfallen expression. "Come on, we'd better eat up. We've still got the rest of the day to get through."

Later that evening, Eve went next door to feed Dog, then drove to a hamburger stand and got dinner for Brice. She got nothing for herself, deciding she wasn't going to stick around to share a meal with him. It was dangerous for her to be alone with him. There was something about him that disturbed her, something about him that made her think thoughts better left unthought.

She hadn't seen him all day, and she couldn't understand the way her heart leapt at the sight of him. As she stepped out on the roof, his face became wreathed in a smile of greeting. His dimples danced in his cheeks like mischievous imps.

"Suppertime," she said briskly, holding out the paper bag of hamburgers and french fries.

"Thanks." He took the bag from her, and she noticed that his hair was damp and the scent of freshly used minty soap clung to him.

"Unless that little tent comes equipped with a shower, you've cheated," she observed.

"Guilty as charged. I snuck down to the boys' locker room and took a fast shower. Come and sit down." He motioned to the sleeping bag where they'd sat on previous nights.

"I really should get back home...." His provocative scent and the warmth of his gaze were sending danger signals to her brain.

"That's one of those bad words you really need to delete from your vocabulary," he chided.

"What word?"

"Should. I should do this, or I should do that. It's one of those binding, limiting words."

"It doesn't matter what words I use, I still need to get right back home."

"Why? What's waiting for you there? Please don't leave yet." He reached out and took her hand. "At least stay until after I eat. The evenings and nights get pretty long up here all alone. I'd really like your company."

Eve couldn't resist the appeal in his voice. Against her better judgment, she allowed him to lead her over to the sleeping bag, where she sat down next to him.

"I feel so isolated up here. Tell me about your day, fill me in," he said as he opened the bag of hamburgers.

She told him a little about her classes, the students who were giving her problems and the ones who were doing well. He was easy to talk to. She wasn't sure if it was the man himself or the setting that made conversation flow effortlessly.

There was something inanely intimate about sharing a rooftop, a feeling of being set apart from the rest of the town, the entire world.

"Johnny Cleavinger really isn't a bad kid, I'm just having trouble reaching him. He's either falling asleep or reading motorcycle magazines in class," Eve finished with a sigh of frustration.

"I was surprised to learn that the school doesn't offer any car-maintenance or engine-repair classes," Brice observed.

"We never had the budget to afford such a class."

"That's too bad. That's probably the kind of thing a boy like Johnny would excel in." Brice offered her a french fry. She accepted it, and he continued talking. "I've seen Johnny and the group of boys he runs with. He and his friends are the ones I'd like to reach." He sighed. "They remind me of me and the gang I used to run with. Hanging out with nothing to do, no way to fill the time, that's how I started on my road to trouble."

"Thank goodness you turned yourself around before you got in too deep," Eve observed, a touch of admiration coloring her tone of voice.

"I still want to get to these kids before they take one step on the road to disaster."

"But how do you reach them?"

Brice grinned. "If I knew that, I wouldn't be sitting up on this roof, I'd be doing whatever it takes to turn these kids around."

Eve pulled her knees up against her chest and wrapped her arms around them, studying him thoughtfully. "What other sort of things did you do to try to reach the kids in New York?"

A sigh whooshed out of him as his brow furrowed. "I tried everything. I staged sit-ins, I rented a hot-air balloon that took the kids on rides, we held dances and pep rallies. For one program I even donned top hat and cane and did a soft-shoe song and dance."

"A soft-shoe?" Eve smiled at the mental picture her mind conjured. He'd probably looked terrific in tails and a top hat. "I would have liked to have seen that."

He nodded, his dimples once again appearing. "It was an ugly sight. It was a personal bet with one of the students. I was horrible, but I won the bet, and the student promised not to drop out of school."

"So you did make a difference there."

"A little, and I want to make a difference here. So many of the problems I had with the students in New York are also here in Pawkinah...the apathy, the lack of commitment, the need for immediate gratification. I want to make a difference here, but I have a feeling I'm bucking a system that doesn't want to change." He looked at her curiously. "Has Mrs. Worthington always run the schools?"

"For as long as I can remember. She has little else in her life. Her husband died years ago, and the school system became her obsession."

"Her ideas are archaic. She runs the school like it's still a one-room building with a dozen students." He paused a moment to pop another french fry into his mouth. "I have a feeling that Mrs. Worthington got more than she bargained for when she hired me."

"I'm surprised she hired you at all," Eve said truthfully.

"My résumé looks good. National test scores rose nearly thirty percent during my time in New York." He paused thoughtfully. "I think Mrs. Worthington had the idea she could control me, despite my track record, and she can—up to a point. But if by standing on my head on Main Street I can motivate the students, then that's exactly what I'm going to do."

Eve nodded, growing thoughtful once again. Only this time her thoughts were not on students or school. Rather, she thought about their previous conversation, and Brice's observations about her family.

"I've been thinking about some of the things you said to me last night," she began tentatively. "I think I'm about ready to make some changes in my life."

Brice's dark eyebrows shot up, and a lazy grin lifted the corners of his mouth. "Does this mean you're ready to crawl into my tent and make passionate love?"

A furious blush warmed Eve's cheeks. "No, that's not what I meant. I'm talking about making changes with my family. I think maybe you're right and I need to step back a little and get some breathing room."

Brice nodded. "I think you'll find that not only will you be happier, but so will your sister and your mother."

"Could I get that in writing?" she asked dryly.

Brice smiled and took her hand in his. As always, at the simple physical contact a wave of warmth swept through her, as if his body heat rushed through his hand to meet hers. "You'll do fine, Eve. Change can be very stimulating."

"What's stimulating to you is terrifying to me," she returned.

"You don't have to be afraid," he said softly. "You won't have to go through anything alone. I'll be right here with you." As he raised her hand up to his lips, Eve knew she was teetering on the edge of falling hopelessly in love with him. And the very thought scared the hell out of her.

The next evening, Eve sat at her kitchen table trying to grade papers, but her mind kept replaying those moments on the roof with Brice.

She was twenty-nine years old, and never in her life had a man affected her so deeply. Never in her life had just sitting next to a man evoked such a tremendous feeling of sensuality. She'd never considered herself an earthy, physical sort of woman, but there was something about Brice that called on a secret place deep inside her, a place nobody else had ever touched.

Dog got up from his resting place at her feet and laid his head on her lap, his mournful eyes looking at her with affection.

"I know, I know, you miss him," she said, scratching the dog behind his good ear.

Dog had awakened her that morning with a heart-rending howl of unhappiness. His howling had remained constant until she went next door and brought him back to her place. So now Fluffy was shut up in the bedroom and Dog had made himself at home by Eve's side.

Strange... Eve had never considered herself a dog person. She'd never much cared for the creatures before. But there was something about Dog that appealed. Like his master, Dog had managed to work his way into a special place in Eve's heart.

She looked at the window, suddenly aware of a strange sound. Dog's ears pricked up, and he whined. Eve got up from the table and went to the window, peering out into the darkness of the night.

Rain... it came out of the sky like an uninvited guest at a birthday party, completely unexpected, and something of a nuisance.

Eve stood at her window and watched the deluge, worry furrowing her brow as she thought of Brice up on the roof of the school. So far, the weather had been cooperative, providing sunny days and warm, starlit nights. She knew he wouldn't call off the deal and leave the roof because it was raining. She also knew he couldn't have prepared for the storm.

She turned away from the window, wondering if his tent was waterproof. Even if it was, he probably didn't have any rain gear, and the night promised to be damp and chilly. The man was just crazy enough to stay up there, ill-prepared, and catch pneumonia.

With an exasperated sigh, she went to the kitchen and opened a can of soup. She poured the contents into a saucepan and placed it on the stove to warm, then left the kitchen and went to the hallway closet. Digging around in the back, she found an old plastic parka. It was cheap but serviceable, a one-size-fits-all that she'd bought years ago to carry with her to outdoor sporting events. She stuffed it into a large tote bag, adding a stadium blanket, then went back in the kitchen and stirred the soup.

Dog sat at her feet, watching curiously as she poured the steaming liquid into a thermos. "I don't want him to get sick," she said, as if needing to rationalize her actions to the animal.

"It's really no big deal," she added as she pulled on her own raincoat and grabbed the thermos and the tote bag. "I'd do it for anyone," she explained to the dog, who cocked his head to one side, as if trying to understand.

Moments later, as she drove to the school, she focused all her attention on the road, finding it difficult to maneuver in the torrent. She parked the car in the school lot and turned off her lights, plunging the area into darkness.

"What are you doing here, Eve?" she asked herself, not moving to get out of the car. What was she doing bringing a rain parka and soup to a man she should have nothing to do with? A man who was as different from her as different could be? What magic was at work, pulling her toward him, mesmerizing her?

Magic, indeed. She scoffed at her own fanciful thoughts. She was just taking some things to her boss, being a good Samaritan. Nothing more, nothing less.

Pulling her raincoat more tightly around her and grabbing the tote bag, she opened the car door and made a mad dash for the stairs that led up to the roof.

The lantern in the tent created a glow that pierced the darkness of the night and the curtain of rain. Eve headed for it like a sailor following the beams of a lighthouse.

For a moment she stood outside the tent, wondering if the rain had washed away the last of her sanity. For surely only insanity could explain her standing on a roof in the middle of a rainstorm on a Saturday night. Surely only insanity could explain why she was even considering entering the intimacy of that tent.

"I'll just throw the things in to him and go back home," she muttered, running one hand through her hair, aware that it was plastered to her scalp. She probably resembled a drowned rat. What did she care if Brice Maxwell got wet? She could turn around and leave and he would never knew she'd been there.

That was exactly what she intended to do, but just then the tent's zipper flew up and Brice's head appeared in the opening. "Eve!" He flashed her that smile that made all reason flee from her mind, all her defenses tumble down. "Come on, get in here before you drown." He opened the flap wider, and before she could gather her wits he pulled her inside.

The interior of the tent was small, so small that physical contact between them was inevitable. He was shirtless, clad only in a pair of tight jeans. His bare, broad shoulder bumping against hers, his muscular thigh rubbing her own, created a tightness in her chest, a weakness in her knees.

"What are you doing here?" he asked incredulously, reaching out to brush the raindrops off the tops of her shoulders. Then his fingers gently swiped the water off her cheeks, his touch seductively warm.

"I...uh...brought you a parka and some warm soup. I didn't know if you had any rain gear or not, and I didn't know if your tent was waterproof or not, and I—" She broke off, aware that she was rambling like a fool. She reached into the tote bag and handed him the items she'd brought.

Oh, this is a mistake, an enormous mistake, she thought helplessly. The tent was so small, so warm and cozy and filled with the masculine scent of him. The lantern cast their shadows on the canvas, further intensifying the intimacy of their surroundings.

It was too much. It was all too much. She shouldn't have come. She should have let him catch pneumonia. With a red, stuffed-up nose and a croupy cough, maybe he wouldn't be so damned attractive.

The tiny tent, Brice's naked chest glowing bronze in the light, his gaze, hot and knowing, silently reaching to meet the desire that burned within her. It was all too much to resist, and when he reached for her she didn't fight, she didn't resist. In fact, she met him halfway, her lips already parted to accept his kiss.

She tasted of raindrops and springtime and smelled of sweet-smelling grass, and Brice felt desire race through him with shuddering intensity. The passion he'd instinctively known she possessed spilled out of her and into him, creating an aching need that he knew nobody but Eve would ever be able to fill.

She reached her hands upward, and for a moment he feared she would push him away, but instead her hands splayed against his chest, moving as if trying to memorize every line, every feature. She sighed into his mouth. It was a sigh of acknowledgment, as if finally she was where she wanted to be. The sigh only increased his desire.

As she caressed him, the dam of self-restraint cracked within him, and with a moan he deepened the kiss, his hands working to remove her raincoat. When he'd succeeded, he pulled his lips from hers and kissed her neck, nipping lightly at the tender, sweet-scented skin. He kissed the base of her neck, where her pulse beat rapidly. A moan of exquisite pleasure escaped her lips, and he pulled back, wanting to look into her eyes, see her face.

Gone was the Eve he had known, with frustration in her bottle-green eyes and tension in her shoulders. It was as if the old Eve had melted away beneath his kiss, exposing a warm, pliant woman whose gaze burned with the fires of desire.

As his lips claimed hers once again, he maneuvered her so that she lay in his arms, breasts to his chest, hip to hip. At the same time, he moved his hands beneath the fleece-lined sweatshirt she wore, cupping her full breasts, silently cursing the cotton bra that kept her flesh from meeting his. Her skin was warm and soft, inviting further caresses.

He pressed his hips against hers, letting her feel how she affected him. At that moment, the wind blew, causing the tent flap to snap open with a sound like a paper bag exploding.

The sound caused Eve to jump, startled.

Brice sat up and looked outside, then zipped the tent flap closed. "It was nothing...just the wind," he whispered, lying back down beside her.

But the noise had jolted Eve out of her haze of passion. She sat up, running a hand through her hair, recriminations taking the place of mindless passion. Dear God, what was she doing? Up on the roof of the building where she was a respectable schoolteacher? What would have happened had it been one of the students checking up on Brice? She was a responsible adult and teacher. She was risking not only her reputation, but her job, as well, by being here with Brice.

"Brice..." She pushed against him as he attempted to put his arms around her once again. "This is madness. We must be crazy."

"You make me crazy," he said, reaching for her yet again. When she failed to respond, his arms fell to his sides.

"I can't... This isn't right." Suddenly her eyes were burning with tears of embarrassment. She felt like a teenage girl who'd gotten in over her head, letting passion overrule good sense.

He sat up beside her and sighed. "You're right. I guess things did get a little out of control." He took her chin in his hand. His eyes were warm, still reflecting the banked fires of desire. "This isn't the time or the place."

"It's not just that," she said, wishing he would stop touching her, stop looking at her with his bedroom eyes. "This whole thing, us... it isn't right."

A smile caused his dimples to dance provocatively in his cheeks. "But it feels so right," he returned softly, his breath a warm caress on the side of her neck.

"Brice, stop it," she protested as he leaned over and kissed her ear. She scooted away from him, immediately feeling bereft as the chill of the outside rain replaced the heat of his body. "I can't be like you, I can't subscribe to the motto 'If it feels good, do it.'" She sighed. It was a heavy one, a sigh of frustration. "We're so different."

His smile deepened, and he reached out and with one finger traced up her arm. "We're supposed to be different. You are woman, I am man."

"You know that's not what I mean." She looked at him—his long hair, his bold features, the confidence that even now radiated from him. He was a man who would never need anyone... and Eve suddenly realized she was a woman who needed to be needed. "Brice, we're like oil and vinegar."

"But if you mix oil and vinegar together you get one hell of a good salad dressing," he countered.

"No matter how much you shake them up, eventually they separate."

"I'll keep us shook up," he returned. Then he sighed in frustration and ran a hand through his hair. "At the moment, I'm more than a little shook."

Eve laid a hand on his arm. "I'm really sorry, Brice. I shouldn't have let things get so out of control." She felt her face color as she continued. "I won't lie to you. I want you. But not like this... It's all too fast."

He grinned crookedly. "Now I'll be honest with you. I've never been a patient man, but I have a feeling you, Eve Winthrop, are worth the wait."

"I would just like for us to get to know each other better before we... uh..." She averted her gaze from his.

"What better way to get to know each other than to make love? Okay, okay..." He laughed good-naturedly at her expression. "We'll take it slow. I should have known a conventional woman like you would want a conventional courtship." He watched as she grabbed her raincoat and slipped it on, belting it tightly at the waist. "How about we plan dinner at my place as soon as I get off this roof?"

Eve shook her head. "I don't think that's such a good idea." Her face colored once again. "I don't think it's a good idea for us to spend any time alone for a while."

He opened him mouth as if to protest, them simply nodded. She moved to the tent flap, ready to crawl out. She paused when he called her name. "I'll walk you to the edge of the roof."

"You don't have to do that, it's still raining," she protested.

"Honey, the second-best thing for me right now is standing in a nice cold rain shower. You want to know what the best thing for me would be?" The wickedness was back in his eyes.

"Absolutely not," Eve answered with a giggle, and she scurried out of the tent and hurried off the roof.

Chapter Seven

Eve stared at the wall that separated her living room from Brice's, trying to figure out what he was doing over there. It sounded like he was having a party. Muted voices, coupled with raucous laughter, drifted through the wall. Occasionally there was a clanging noise, like a hammer being applied to metal pipes.

She redirected her attention to the book in her hands, trying to ignore the sounds of revelry. If Brice was having a party, that was his business. It was early evening on a Saturday night, not late enough for the noise to be really bothersome.

She sighed and tugged on her hair, trying to concentrate on the words in front of her. However, it was difficult to concentrate on anything when her thoughts were filled with Brice.

He'd finally gotten off the roof last Tuesday, when
the attendance had fallen and several students had
been absent. For the past week, Eve had maintained a
healthy distance from him, realizing that she was vulnerable to him. She had no sense where he was concerned. Her brain switched off and her hormones
kicked in every time he was around. Luckily, he had
been busy all week, so he'd had very little time for
personal contact with her.

But just because they hadn't had any time together
since the night they had almost made love in his tent,
that didn't mean there wasn't anything happening between them.

All he had to do was gaze at her across the crowded
lunchroom and her mouth went dry and a warm tin-
gling began in the pit of her stomach. Bumping
shoulders with him in the hallway, hearing his deep
laughter drift out of his office, watching him interact
with a group of students, all made her feel light-
headed, weak-kneed. She couldn't forget the way he'd
made her feel when she was in his arms, so wonderfully alive. It was a feeling she thought might be ad-
dictive.

She jumped when a knock rapped at her door. She
answered it, and there he stood, bigger than life. He
was dressed in a pair of jeans and a short-sleeved
denim shirt that loved the width of his shoulders. His
dark hair was as wild as a warrior's, and she instantly
had to stifle an impulse to reach out and run her hand

through it. His eyes were those of a mischievous boy, and his smile reflected some inner excitement.

"Do you have any popcorn I could borrow?" he asked.

"I think so," she replied, opening the door wider so that he could step inside. She went into the kitchen, found a bag of popcorn, then returned to where he waited. "Here you go."

"Thanks," he said, taking the popcorn and leaving before she had a chance to say anything more.

She closed her door, shaking her head in bewilderment. What on earth was he doing over there?

She'd just settled back on the sofa when once again a knock fell on her door. She opened it to see Brice smiling broadly. "Do you have any butter?"

She nodded, hurrying to the kitchen. "What are you doing over there?" she asked a moment later as she handed him a stick of butter.

"Come on over and find out," he said with a mysterious grin.

"Oh, no, it's really none of my—"

"Come on," he interrupted, grabbing her hand and tugging her across the porch and through his front door.

"Hi, Miss Winthrop." Johnny Cleavinger and four of his friends sat in a circle on Brice's living room floor. At the center of the circle, laid out on a sheet, were the parts of a motorcycle.

Eve turned to Brice anxiously. "That's—that's not your motorcycle, is it?"

He grinned, obviously pleased with himself. "No, it's one I bought down at the junkyard. The boys here are going to spend their Saturday nights putting it back together."

"Yeah, and once we've got it all in shape we're going to auction it off and use the money for a school dance." Johnny's face held more animation, more excitement, than Eve had ever seen there. His friends' faces mirrored his own. "Isn't it awesome?" he finished with a wide grin.

"Of course, the guys have promised me that in return for getting to come here on Saturday nights they'll work to get their grades up," Brice explained.

Eve smiled at him warmly. These boys were some of the at-risk students, destined for dropout or failure. But he'd managed to discover a way to reach these boys and motivate them. Her heart filled with pride in him.

"You guys hang loose, and I'll go make us some popcorn," Brice said, moving toward the kitchen.

Eve touched his arm. "If I wouldn't be cramping your style, infringing on the rites of male bonding, I'd be glad to make the popcorn."

"You don't have to do that," he protested.

"I'd like to," she answered simply. It was true. She wanted to do something to help him with his project. "I want to help. I don't know anything about engines and motorcycles, but I can make a mean bowl of popcorn."

He handed her the stick of butter. "Thanks." His smile was so warm it caused an answering warmth to flood through her, making her fear the butter would melt right out of her hand.

"One bowl of popcorn coming right up," she murmured, escaping into the kitchen with a breathless sigh.

At least she didn't have to worry about things getting out of control with Brice, not with five teenage chaperons around.

With that comforting thought in mind she headed for the stove, where a large saucepan, a bottle of oil and the bag of popcorn awaited her. Dog ambled his way in and sat down at her feet, looking at her with mournful eyes that begged her to drop a morsel or two his way.

Nearly half an hour later, Eve still stood in the kitchen, popping the last pan of popcorn. The bowl in the living room had emptied as fast as she had filled it. She had never known that teenage boys had such voracious appetites.

She smiled, waiting for the kernels to start exploding. She really didn't mind standing over the hot stove, jiggling the saucepan back and forth over and over again.

In fact, she was finding the experience quite pleasant. There was something nice about standing in the kitchen, cooking up treats, while laughter and camaraderie reigned in the next room. She could hear Brice's low voice, then his rumbling laughter. He was so good with the kids, able to converse with them on their level and not sound condescending. It was obvious he genuinely liked them, and the boys responded to him in kind.

He would make a wonderful father. The thought struck her suddenly. It was easy to envision him wrestling in the other room with a couple of toddlers, his deep laughter mingling with their squeals of delight. He would be the kind of father who always had time for his children, a man who would bond with them as effortlessly as a cow moos. The vision of him with a couple of children caused a lump to appear in her throat and a warm, fuzzy feeling to explode in her chest.

She jumped as the kernels began to pop, pulling her from her crazy imaginings. She shook her head ruefully. Brice Maxwell might make a terrific father, but he'd probably make a horrid husband. Of course, she had no real reason for this supposition, except that it was a good defense against her growing feelings for him.

She finished popping the corn and carried the pan out to the living room, where the guys were having a lively discussion about pistons and crankshafts. "Last bowl," she announced. "I reached the bottom of the bag."

There was a chorus of good-natured groans. She handed the pan to Johnny, then headed for the front door. "Well, I guess I'll leave you guys alone," she said.

"Don't go," Brice protested, moving out of the recliner chair to stop her. "We could use a feminine presence to keep us all in line." He took her arm and, despite her sputtering protests, led her to his chair, his actions accompanied by encouraging laughter from the boys.

With a helpless laugh of surrender, she allowed Brice to push her back into his chair. He joined the boys on the blanket, and the talk immediately went back to engines and motorcycles.

Eve settled back in relaxation, smiling as Dog walked over and lay down at her feet. She'd "accidentally" dropped more than a couple of pieces of popcorn on the floor for Dog's benefit, and he was now ready for a snooze, his stomach full.

For the next hour, she sat and listened to the boys and Brice talking. She understood little of the conversation, which was peppered with mechanical terms. Still, she found it enjoyable. She had all five boys in her English classes, and never had she heard them talk so much or look so lively. It was nice seeing them outside the structure of the class. It gave her a different perspective on each one. She also enjoyed watching Brice, who looked so boyish, so warm and alive, as he teased first one, then another, of the teens.

"I think a dance is a dumb idea," Carl Witherspoon, a lanky blond, suddenly announced.

"Ah, that's just because you don't know how to dance," Johnny said, teasing his friend.

Jeff Majors, another of the boys laughed. "Yeah, you probably have two left feet."

"So, who cares about dancing?" Carl returned defiantly, his face reddening with a flush of embarrassment. "I think dancing is dumb."

"I don't know how to dance," Bobby Macomb admitted, his cherub face offering a shy smile. "Maybe Miss Winthrop could teach us. All girls know how to dance."

Six pairs of eyes turned to look at Eve.

She squirmed beneath their gazes. "Oh...I can't... I mean, I don't..."

"That's a great idea," Brice exclaimed, jumping up and heading for the stereo. "I've got all kinds of music here...." He began pulling out records. "We've got Latin beat, disco, rock and roll...."

As one, the boys all voiced their preference. "Rock and roll."

"Really, I can't," Eve protested.

"Of course you can," Brice returned, placing the records on the turntable, then pulling her out of the chair. "Just dance with me," he whispered as an upbeat fifties tune began to play.

He was a good dancer. The natural grace Eve had admired about him many times was apparent as he moved to the beat of the music. He danced as he did everything, with enormous enthusiasm and energy, without an ounce of self-consciousness. Eve found her own self-consciousness fading away beneath the warmth of his smile.

"Come on, guys, you can at least give it a try," she said to the boys, who were still sitting and watching. "All you have to do is move to the beat."

Johnny jumped up and joined Brice and Eve, making them laugh as he moonwalked across the room.

Before long, all the boys were up on their feet, trying to mimic Eve's and Brice's movements. Johnny showed his friends and the adults the steps of some of the newest dances, and Brice and Eve showed the boys the steps to some old dances.

Eve laughed until her sides ached as Brice did the swim, the pony, and several other once-popular steps that now looked ridiculous. She took turns dancing with first one, then another, patiently showing them steps, laughing with them at their mistakes and her own.

It was almost midnight when Brice shut off the stereo and announced that it was time for the boys to go home. His announcement was met with a chorus of groans, but the kids didn't argue. When they left, they were already talking about what they wanted to accomplish on the motorcycle the next Saturday night.

Eve started out behind them, not wanting to be left alone with him. She knew better than to trust her own defenses.

"Whoa! Where are you running to?" Brice asked as she moved toward the front door.

"I've got to get home." She smiled. "All the laughter has exhausted me."

He moved to stand next to her, an answering smile on his face. "I like to hear you laugh. You should do it more often."

"If you'd do those dopey dances more often, I'd certainly laugh more." She shook her head. "I can't believe we actually did those crazy steps and thought we were cool."

"If you want to see my skillful renditions of the monkey and the stroll, I suggest you come back next week." His grin faded, and he looked at her more seriously. "Actually, I hope you will come back next week. I think it's good to have a female here for the boys to relate to on a more casual basis."

Eve nodded. "I'd like to come back."

He leaned forward and ran a finger down the side of her face. "How about a cup of coffee? If you'll stay, I'll be glad to make some...in the morning." He winked suggestively.

Eve tapped his shoulder lightly in admonition. "How about I meet you in the morning about nine out on the porch for a cup of your coffee?"

"My way sounds more exciting," he countered.

"But my way is more apt to happen," she returned with an easy smile.

He laughed in defeat. "All right, coffee on the porch at nine." Before she realized his intent, he leaned over and kissed her softly on the forehead. "Pleasant dreams, Eve."

She nodded, backing out of his duplex. She turned and hurried into her own place, where she breathed a sigh of longing. Oh, it was hard to maintain distance from Brice. He was a difficult man to keep out of her heart. It was a battle she feared she was losing.

At precisely nine o'clock the next morning, Eve stepped out of her duplex and sat down on the front porch, breathing in the sweet-scented morning air. It was a gorgeous morning. The sky was blue, and the sun was warm overhead. She wasn't sure if it was particularly pretty in reality or if she just thought so because she was going to be sharing it with Brice. Before she'd even had a chance to get completely comfortable on the concrete stoop, Brice's door swung open and he appeared, carrying a tray with coffee for two.

"Good morning," he said, carefully balancing the tray as he sat down beside her.

"Good morning," she returned, smiling warmly.

"I hope you like my coffee. It's a special blend." He handed her a cup of the steaming brew.

Eve took an experimental sip, pleasantly surprised by the burst of chocolate and cinnamon flavoring mingled with the coffee taste. "This is delicious."

"It usually tastes better if it's served in bed." His eyes sparkled attractively.

"I don't think it could taste better than it does at this moment," she returned, making him chuckle.

"You are one stubborn woman, Eve Winthrop."

"I'm a careful woman," Eve countered, taking another drink of her coffee.

"Sometimes I think you are too careful."

"And sometimes I think you are too impetuous," Eve returned.

"So where does that leave us?" he asked.

"Just having coffee on the porch." She smiled again and raised her face up to the warmth of the morning sun. "I refuse to banter with you this morning, Brice. It takes too much energy, and I'm feeling sinfully lazy."

"Hmm...too bad you aren't just feeling sinful," he grumbled, sipping his coffee.

For a few minutes they sat there, drinking their coffee and enjoying the tranquillity of the morning. It was one of the few truly gorgeous spring days Pawkinah had to offer. The sky was a cloudless blue, the trees were displaying their new green foliage, and the air carried the scent of pungent flowers.

"It's so quiet here," Brice said, draining his mug and setting it on the stoop next to him.

"It must be quite different from New York," she observed.

Brice laughed. "There's no comparison. There's no such thing as quiet in New York City. You function on sensory overload all the time."

"Sounds horrible."

"Actually, it's not," he explained. "There's something exciting about it. It's like feeling the pulse beating in your veins all the time. It's drama every day, excitement every minute."

"You sound like you miss it."

"Not really." He stretched his long legs out in front of him. "The noise, the excitement, the drama of New York City was great, but when I accepted the job here it was because I was ready for a change. Besides—" he leaned back and looked around the quiet neighborhood "—New York City is no place to raise kids."

Eve lifted her eyebrows and looked at him. "Are you planning on raising kids?" Her heart began an unsteady tattoo in her chest.

"Eventually. What about you? Do you want a family?"

"I haven't given it much thought." Eve flushed suddenly as she remembered her momentary fantasy the night before, standing in his kitchen imagining him in the living room with a couple of toddlers. "Yes, eventually I'd like a family," she answered. "Although I have some other family matters to take care of before I move on with my personal life."

"How are things going with your mother and your sister?"

Eve smiled reflectively and finished her coffee. "I'm finding that it's difficult to say no."

"You have no problem in that respect where I'm concerned," he teased, the warmth of his azure eyes washing over her.

"You know what I mean." She elbowed him lightly in the side, then continued. "Old habits die hard, and it's been my habit to always be available for my family, to never say no when they want or need something. But I am starting to make changes." She grinned at him. "I'm even starting to live danger-ously."

"How so?" he asked, his dark eyebrows dancing upward on his forehead.

"I bought a new jacket yesterday, and I didn't write my name in the collar."

Brice laughed. "If you don't watch out, you might really become crazy and impulsive, and it will be you staging a sit-in on top of the school building."

Eve smiled dubiously. "It would have to be an aw-fully important issue to resort to such drastic mea-sures."

"Speaking of important issues—" Brice looked at his wristwatch "—I've got to get moving. I've got a friend flying into Oklahoma City for a conference. I'm driving there to visit with him for a little while to-night."

"That's a good three-hour drive," Eve observed, standing up when he did. "He must be a good friend."

"He is. We went through college together, room-mates. We don't get much chance to see each other." He took the coffee cup she handed him.

"Thanks for the coffee, and drive safely." She hated the thought of him driving that distance on his mo-torcycle, and her worry must have shown in her eyes.

"I'll be fine," he assured her. "And I'll see you in the morning at school."

She nodded, watching as he grabbed the cups and tray and disappeared into his duplex.

She sat down on the porch again, wondering if it was just her imagination or if the brilliance of the morning hadn't dimmed somewhat when he'd gone inside.

Was it possible that Brice somehow had that power over her? That when he was with her the sky was bluer, the air sweeter, life more exciting? She shivered and stood up, refusing to delve into the ramifications of such thoughts.

It was much later in the day when Colleen stopped by to return the blue dress she had borrowed.

"It needs to be cleaned. I dropped a little glob of cocktail sauce on the front," Colleen explained, carrying the dress with her into Eve's bedroom. "I'd like to borrow another one. Mrs. Worthington has a dinner for some charity thing this Wednesday night, and she wants me to go with her, but I don't have anything to wear."

"Sure, just let me know which one you're borrowing." Eve resumed her position on the sofa, where she'd been relaxing for a few minutes before Colleen arrived.

"I came by last night, but you weren't home." Colleen's voice drifted out of the bedroom, along with the sounds of hangers clicking together as she rummaged through Eve's closet.

"I was next door." Eve smiled as she thought about her evening with Brice and the kids.

"Next door?" Colleen leaned her head out the doorway. "You mean at Brice Maxwell's? What were you doing over there?"

"He invited some of the kids over, and we're all working on a secret project," Eve replied with a grin.

"A secret project? What kind of a secret project?"

Eve grinned. "Now, it wouldn't be a secret if I told you, would it?"

Colleen scowled and disappeared once again into the bedroom.

"Hey, where did you get this cute little peach silk?" Colleen called once again from the bedroom.

This comment pulled Eve off the sofa and into the bedroom, where Colleen had tossed several of Eve's dresses on the bed. She was holding up a melon-colored silk dress that still had a price tag dangling from an underarm.

"This is darling," Colleen exclaimed, holding the dress before her and twirling around in front of the mirror. "Where'd you get it?"

"I bought it a couple months ago at that little boutique down on Main." It had been a whim. She'd been shopping for a new work outfit and had seen this dress and loved it. After trying it on, even knowing that it was a ridiculously indulgent purchase, far too dressy to wear to work, she'd bought it. She'd shoved it into the back of her closet, hoping that someday she would need a very special dress to wear for a very special man. "I'd rather you not borrow that one," Eve said.

"But this is the one I want. It would look great on me," Colleen protested, once again turning to the mirror and admiring her reflection.

"If you notice, the price tag is still on it. I haven't even worn it yet."

"Where do you ever go that you could wear a dress as fancy and pretty as this one? You might as well let me get some use out of it."

"No." Eve said the word quietly, but firmly. She took the dress out of her sister's hands and hung it back in the closet. "I have several others that are almost as nice. You're welcome to borrow any of them." She picked up the blue dress that Colleen had brought back and handed it to her. "Also, you can return this to me after you have it cleaned."

Colleen stared at Eve as if she'd grown a second head. "Gosh, what's the matter with you? Did you have a bad week at school, or what?"

"Nothing's wrong with me. I just think it's fair that you clean the dress. After all, you spilled on it."

"You've never made me clean the things I borrowed before," Colleen exclaimed, still looking at Eve in amazement. "Why are you being so mean?"

"I'm not being mean, I'm being fair. I always pay for the cleaning when you borrow something of mine, and that isn't right." Eve smiled gently at her sister. "Now, what about my black dress with the silver buttons for this charity thing with Mrs. Worthington? That outfit always looks nice on you."

"Forget it, I'll wear something of my own." Colleen snapped. "I don't know why you're being so darned mean." Eve followed her sister as she stomped out of the room and to the front door. "I'll bring back the blue one after it's cleaned, but I think you're being hateful."

With that, Colleen slammed out of the house.

Eve sighed, hoping Colleen's anger wouldn't last long. Eve didn't like to fight with her sister. Still, she couldn't help but feel good about what had just transpired. It had been the first battle in what would probably be a long war. But she'd been victorious. She'd said no.

Eve wished she could rush right next door and tell Brice what she had done. It wasn't much, but it was a beginning. She'd taken a stand and stuck to her guns, and she felt wonderful.

But Brice wasn't home yet from his trip to Oklahoma City, and as the evening lengthened and night fell, he still didn't return home.

When ten o'clock came, Eve made herself go to bed, trying not to worry about the fact that Brice had still not returned. It seemed strange, to worry about somebody other than her immediate family—strange, but nice. She'd spent so much of her time in the past three years worrying about her mom and Colleen that the idea of caring about somebody else was nice for a change.

It wasn't until midnight, when she heard the throb of his motorcycle in the garage and she knew he was home safe and sound, that she was able to close her eyes and fall sound asleep.

Chapter Eight

"It's unbelievable," Susan Birch, the science teacher announced, sitting down next to Margie and Eve at the lunch table in the teachers' lounge.

"What's so unbelievable?" Margie asked curiously.

Susan opened her brown bag and withdrew a sandwich and an apple, shaking her head in amazement. "Today, after class, Angela Baker came up to me and asked if she could do some extra credit work to help her grade so she'd get to join the rooftop club. Angela Baker! That girl hasn't shown an interest in anything except makeup and boys all year. Now, suddenly, she wants extra credit assignments."

"It's the rooftop club," Margie said. "All the kids are talking about it."

"Personally, I think it's the greatest thing since sliced bread," Susan returned. "Anything that gets the kids motivated is okay in my book."

"The kids have been wild since Mr. Maxwell announced his intention to have an end-of-the-year dance," Margie commented.

"I think that's great, too," Susan said, biting into her sandwich and pausing a moment to chew. "I think it's shameful that these kids haven't been able to have a dance for the last five years. Dances and high school go together like...like...pastrami and rye!" she finished, holding out her sandwich to make her point.

Eve smiled, thinking over the past two weeks. True to his words, Brice had established his rooftop club, serving pizza and soft drinks once a week on the roof to the students who'd shown the most improvement in their classes. He'd then made the announcement about the dance, inspiring even more excitement among the students.

These weren't the only changes that had generated some excitement among the students over the past couple of weeks. Brice had also announced that he intended to ask the school board to allocate funds for a computer lab. This news had been greeted enthusiastically, not only by the students, but by most of the teachers, as well.

Still, there were other things that had happened recently that made a smile easier to come by for Eve. Slowly she had been withdrawing from her mother and her sister, not being as readily available to their demands, encouraging them to be more independent. And the end result was a sense of freedom, a rediscovering of herself, that was exhilarating.

"I heard a very strange rumor yesterday," Margie said the moment Susan had finished eating and left the table.

"What kind of a rumor?" Eve asked curiously.

"I heard through the grapevine that you and Mr. Maxwell were having a hot relationship."

"That's ridiculous," Eve scoffed, aware that her reddening cheeks belied her protest.

"Rumor has it that you've been spending Saturday nights at his place, indulging in a wild, passionate affair."

Eve laughed, despite her initial outrage. She couldn't help but laugh. The gossip mongers had certainly been busy. Unfortunately, they'd gotten their wires crossed and played liberally with the truth in this matter.

"Margie, that's the most ridiculous thing I've ever heard," she exclaimed. She laughed at the total absurdity of the story. "Actually, I have been spending Saturday nights at Brice's place."

Margie's eyes glittered brightly and she leaned toward Eve eagerly. "And—?"

"So has Johnny Cleavinger, and four of his closest friends. They've been rebuilding a motorcycle, and I've been acting like a kind of den mother, dispensing popcorn and female advice for their benefit."

Margie's face fell. "I knew the story wasn't half as juicy as it sounded. Gossip never is." She sighed and stood up. "Well, I'd better get to class. I promised Billy Slolom I'd meet with him a few minutes after lunch to help him with his art project."

It wasn't until Margie had left and Eve was alone that she thought back over the last couple of Saturday nights. Actually, the story was a bit juicier than she'd let on. But it would have been impossible to explain to an outsider the subtle nuances, the tensions, that existed between Brice and herself. The anticipation of his touch, the seductive warmth of his gaze, the frustration of knowing that the desire they felt for each other could not be expressed physically. All these things were a part of the Saturday-night meetings, a part she wasn't willing to share with anyone. It was all too wonderful, all too new, for her to want to share it.

She finished her lunch and left the lounge, heading for the office to check her mailbox. She greeted the secretary with a friendly smile. "Hi, Ann."

"Hi, Eve." Ann returned the smile, shuffling a stack of papers from one side of the desk to the other. "Your sister was in early this morning."

"She was?" Eve frowned, wondering what Colleen had been doing at the school. "She was probably running errands for Mrs. Worthington," Eve said, speaking her thoughts aloud.

"I think she put a message in your box."

"She did?" Eve crossed the office to the built-in mailboxes along one wall. Reaching into hers, she withdrew a handful of notes and phone messages. She quickly scanned the notes, her heart thudding to a halt as she read the one she assumed Colleen had delivered. It was an invitation—no, a direct summons for Eve to go to Mrs. Worthington's home immediately after school.

"Everything all right?" Ann asked.

"Oh, fine," Eve answered absently. Telling Ann goodbye, she headed back to her classroom, worry lines furrowing her forehead.

Why did Mrs. Worthington want to see her? She'd never been asked to meet with the woman before. What could she possibly want?

She still had no answers that afternoon, when she got into her car and headed toward Mrs. Worthington's imposing home.

The Worthington mansion was set at the north edge of the small town, a huge southern plantation-style home in the middle of five carefully manicured acres.

Irene Worthington had never been one to socialize with the teachers, so Eve had never been inside the impressive house.

She pulled into the circular driveway and shut off the car's engine, sitting for a moment to calm her unsteady nerves. There was something ominous about this whole thing. Eve had been teaching in the Pawkinah school system for over five years, and never had she been asked to meet with Mrs. Worthington. Why, suddenly, did the old woman want to see her now?

Taking a deep breath, she climbed out of the car and nervously smoothed down the front of her skirt. She approached the massive front door and rang the bell, hearing distant, resounding chimes echoing somewhere within.

"Ah, Eve, so nice of you to drop by," Irene said as she greeted her at the door. As always, the woman was impeccably dressed, in a tailored suit that made her overweight body look distinguished rather than fat. Her hair looked as if she'd just stepped out of an expensive salon, and the perfume that wafted from her smelled rich.

Eve smiled. Drop by... As if she'd had a choice in the matter. When the queen summoned, the peasants scurried.

"Please, come in." She ushered Eve into the foyer, which was the size of Eve's living room. Eve couldn't help but feel slightly intimidated by this physical proof of wealth and power.

"Please, let's go into the library, where we'll be more cozy."

She followed the woman into a room Eve would hardly have described as "cozy." Even the rich oak paneling and shelves of books couldn't warm the cold, sterile atmosphere.

Mrs. Worthington took a seat behind a large oak desk and motioned for Eve to sit on the straight-backed chair before her.

Eve sat down, wondering why she suddenly had the feeling that she was about to undergo a line of questioning that would make the Inquisition look mild.

"How are things going at the school?" Mrs. Worthington asked pleasantly.

"Fine, although things always get somewhat hectic when we are approaching the end of the year," Eve answered truthfully.

"The reason I asked you to come here today is that I've heard some rumors that have me quite concerned."

The same rumors that Margie had heard? Eve wondered, her heart immediately clutching in her chest. Was there a morality clause in their contracts? Was there a policy against teachers and principals seeing each other on a social basis? "Rumors?" she asked, her mouth suddenly dry with anxiety.

Mrs. Worthington nodded. "Unsettling things that have me quite concerned as to the direction Mr. Maxwell is taking our school. For one thing, I've heard he's planning a dance."

Eve expelled a soft sigh of relief. "Yes, I believe he has mentioned the possibility of a dance. The students are quite excited about it."

Mrs. Worthington's nostrils flared slightly. "Of course the students would be excited. They don't have the wisdom to know what's best for themselves." She sighed heavily. "I thought I had made it clear to Mr. Maxwell that dances were not necessary... not acceptable." She frowned, causing the wrinkles in her forehead to intensify so that they resembled several inverted question marks. "I've also received word that Mr. Maxwell wants a computer lab."

Eve mumbled a noncommittal reply, wondering why she had been called here to listen to Mrs. Worthington's litany of complaints against Brice.

"I can't understand why Mr. Maxwell hasn't been able to grasp that all we want is for him to focus on the basics—reading, writing and arithmetic. Oh, well, I'm digressing." She waved her hands impatiently. "The real reason I invited you here is because I understand that you live next door to Mr. Maxwell."

Eve nodded, suddenly wary.

Mrs. Worthington leaned forward, her facial features shifting to accommodate a conspiratorial smile. "Eve, I really don't think Brice Maxwell is what we need here in Pawkinah. Certainly I take partial responsibility for not checking more carefully the personal qualifications of the man. However, I certainly didn't expect a man with his professional qualifications to look and act like such a—a hooligan."

Eve couldn't help but smile at the use of the old-fashioned word. "Mr. Maxwell *is* rather unconventional," she agreed.

"Exactly my point." Mrs. Worthington smiled in delight. "I'm so glad you agree with my opinion. Now, what I would like for you to do is keep an eye on Mr. Maxwell. I understand he's been inviting students to his house. I'd like to know who those students are and exactly what they are doing there. I'd also like to know if he's having contact with any other members of the school board."

Eve looked at the older woman with confusion. "I'm not sure I understand. Are you asking me to spy on Mr. Maxwell?" Eve was surprised at the immediate, violent sense of outrage that rushed through her. And in her outrage she realized something both wonderful and dreadful. She loved Brice Maxwell, and she would do everything in her power to fight this woman who she sensed was a threat to him.

"Now, Eve, *spy* is such a distasteful word," Mrs. Worthington protested. "I simply want what's best for the students, and I'm not thoroughly convinced that Brice Maxwell is the man for this town." She smiled once again. "I'm simply attempting to gather information, find out what the general response is to Mr. Maxwell's unusual methods. I'd like to know what his plans are for the future so that I might address any problems that could arise."

"If you want to know about Mr. Maxwell's future plans, then I suggest you ask Mr. Maxwell. I won't be a party to spying and reporting on his activities," Eve returned stiffly.

Mrs. Worthington stood up with a frown. "I'm sorry we don't see eye-to-eye on this particular issue. I know many of the parents and students hold you in high esteem. I'm not sure the same can be said for Brice Maxwell. Good day, Miss Winthrop."

Eve stood up, also, realizing she was being dismissed. With a mumbled goodbye, she left. Once back outside, she got into her car and drove home as quickly as possible, her only thought to get to Brice and tell him what had just transpired between her and the senior member of the school board.

He answered his door on the second knock. Wearing a pair of cutoff jean shorts and a T-shirt, he held a skillet in his hand, letting Eve know she had interrupted his dinner preparations.

"You're just in time," he announced, his smile telling of his pleasure at the sight of her. "In fifteen minutes you can taste a sample of my culinary delights."

"I need to talk to you," she said, following him from the front door into the kitchen. "I think Mrs. Worthington is trying to gather information to get rid of you."

Brice grinned unconcernedly and placed the skillet on the stove. With deft movements, he cut off a portion of a stick of butter, plopped it in the skillet, then added a bowl of sliced fresh mushrooms.

"Brice, did you hear me?"

"I heard you." He waited until the mushrooms were simmering, then plopped a lid on the pan and turned to her with a smile. "And I'm really not surprised. Irene Worthington has made it quite clear from the very beginning that I wasn't exactly her idea of an ideal civil servant."

Eve paced the kitchen floor anxiously. "We have to do something . . . stop her."

"What do you suggest?" He pushed her into a kitchen chair while giving her a gentle smile, then sat down in the seat across from her. "What do you suggest, Eve?" he repeated. "That I cut my hair, buy some Brooks Brothers suits? Do you want me to stop all the programs I have implemented, cancel my plans for a dance?"

"A haircut would be a start," Eve said, but she didn't mean it. She didn't want Brice to cut his hair. The longer length was part of him, part of what made him who he was.

He reached across the table and took her hand in his. "Do you really think the length of my hair would make any real difference with Mrs. Worthington?"

"Probably not," Eve agreed. "But we have to do something. We can't just let you lose your job here. Maybe if you talked to her, worked out some sort of compromise..."

"The woman doesn't know the meaning of the word," he said dryly. "No, there's nothing to be done." He got up and stirred the mushrooms, then opened the oven door and took a covered pan out and set it on the counter. "I've got smothered steak, a big salad, and a loaf of French bread. You'll stay and eat with me?"

Eve paused a moment, then nodded absently. She didn't want to leave here until she knew they had a plan of action to stymie Mrs. Worthington. "What can I do to help?"

"You can set the table. The plates are in that cabinet, and the silverware is in the drawer next to the sink."

"I meant with Mrs. Worthington," she explained.

"Dinner first," he commanded, pointing to the cabinet where he kept his dishes.

As she set the table, Brice completed the dinner preparations, and within minutes the meal was on the table and ready to eat.

"This is delicious," Eve announced after taking a bite of the mushroom-covered steak. "Where did you learn to cook like this?"

"Trial and error," he explained. "I've been a bachelor a lot of years, and it was either learn how to cook or eat out all the time."

"Why haven't you married?" Eve asked, immediately feeling a blush rise to her face at the personal question. Still, she'd wondered about it a million times since getting to know him. She couldn't believe some woman hadn't captured his heart years before.

He chewed thoughtfully for a moment before answering. "I guess marriage has never been a top priority with me," he began. "I've had several relationships, but when it came to making that leap into wedded bliss, I've always gotten cold feet." He paused, his forehead wrinkled in thought. "I guess it's always been important to me to retain my independence. I worked so hard to get it, and I never wanted to depend on anyone. It took me too many years to learn not to depend on other people."

Eve nodded, her heart dropping an inch lower in her chest at his words. They simply confirmed the fact that she was crazy even to consider a relationship between herself and Brice. He was telling her in a roundabout way that he wasn't willing to give enough of himself to sustain a long-term relationship. She'd been duly warned. Too bad her heart didn't have ears.

She focused on her steak, not wanting him to see the emotion in her heart reflected in her eyes.

"How are things going with your family?" he asked, his casual tone letting her know he sensed nothing amiss.

"Fine. Actually, better than fine." Eve smiled at him. "Oh, there are still some battles to be won, but I think, generally speaking, I've won the war." She smiled. "I even talked Mom into joining a bridge club. She's having a ball." She looked at him shyly. "I owe you a debt of gratitude. If you hadn't pointed out the problems, I probably would have let things continue as they were, and I would have grown more and more depressed and not known why."

"I don't believe that," Brice protested. "You're an intelligent woman. Eventually you would have realized some changes needed to be made." His eyes sparked with a sensual warmth. "Of course, you could still use some more adjustments, especially in the area of risk-taking."

"I'm making adjustments in that area," Eve said with a laugh. "I'm having dinner here with you now, and that's a risk I wasn't willing to take before now."

The twinkle in his eyes sparked brighter. "If you really want to take a risk, you'll hang around after dinner and have a glass of wine with me." There was a definite challenge in his smile.

"White or red?" Eve answered, with a recklessness she hoped she wouldn't regret.

"Do you realize this is the first time we've been completely alone since my rooftop escapade?" Brice asked moments later, as they sat on the living room floor.

Eve nodded, very much aware of the fact that they were alone, that he was sitting so close to her that she could feel the heat emanating from his body, smell the scent that belonged to him alone. She took a sip of her wine, hoping the chilled liquid would cool the tempestuous thoughts in her head. "Why don't you have a sofa?" she asked, trying to steer the conversation away from the fact that they were alone together.

"I had one in New York, an ugly plaid thing. When I got ready to pack everything up and move, I realized it wasn't worth the trouble. I had planned to buy a new one as soon as I got settled in, but I haven't taken the time. Besides—" he scooted over closer to her and placed an arm around her shoulders "—there's something to be said for the convenience and comfort of a thickly carpeted floor. Have you ever felt the sensation of a plush rug against your bare skin?"

"Have you ever felt the sensation of a glass of wine poured over your head?" Eve returned with a giggle. Then she sobered, and turned the conversation back to the original reason she had come by. "Brice, I wish you'd take more seriously this mess with Mrs. Worthington."

"The only thing I really want to take seriously right now is you." His eyes smoldered like blue fire, and his hand reached up to play in her hair.

Eve looked away, refusing to fall into the flames of stirring desire that danced in his azure gaze. "Maybe I could get up a petition or something like that on your behalf," she said, staring at the wall before her.

"Eve." Brice set his wineglass down and moved so that he was sitting directly in front of her. He placed his hands on either side of her face. The light of desire was gone from his eyes now. "The problem with Mrs. Worthington is not your problem. It's mine, and I've told you before, I take care of my own messes."

"Yes, but—"

Her protest was cut off by Brice's lips claiming hers. His mouth tasted of wine, sweet and hot, and even though Eve knew it was foolish, she responded, eagerly opening her lips to accept the kiss. He somehow managed to take her wineglass from her and set it on the floor near them. Then he wrapped his arms around her, enfolding her so close that she could feel his heart beating fast and furious, in his chest, echoing her own.

His lips played against hers with an expertise that left her breathless, gasping for more. With a graceful agility, he eased her backward and down on the carpet, his body covering hers like a warm, comfortable blanket. His lips took hers hungrily, with a maddening skill that stole what protests she might have wanted to make.

At the same time his mouth was making magic against hers, his hands moved up beneath her blouse, stroking her rib cage, moving across her stomach, then upward, toward her breasts. With an easy flick of his fingers, he released the front catch of her bra, moaning deep in his throat as he covered her breasts with his warm palms.

Eve answered his moan with one of her own. She felt his hunger in his touch, in his kiss, and she realized it was calling on the hunger in her. She cried out in pleasure as his mouth left her lips and settled along the side of her neck, where he rained teasing nips that caused shivers of pleasure to dance up her spine.

She wanted him, and she didn't care about tomorrow, she didn't care about anything but her love for him.

"Oh, my sweet Eve," he murmured, his hands working the blouse up and over her head and pushing her bra off her shoulders. He took a moment to pull his T-shirt off, then enfolded her close once again.

Eve shivered convulsively at the contact of her breasts rubbing against the thick hair that covered his chest. The springy hair rubbed erotically against her taut nipples. He moved his lips to cover their tautness, teasing the rosy tips of each breast in turn. Eve tangled her hands in his hair, pulling him closer. "Yes," she whispered as his tongue ravished her.

His hands moved down to grip her buttocks and pull her to him. She could feel his arousal, hard and insistent beneath his jean shorts, pressing against her, demanding attention. She moved her hips against his, catching her breath as he groaned into her neck. Her hands moved down his muscled back, enjoying the tactile sensation of his hot flesh beneath her palms. He groaned into her neck, his breath hot and erotic.

Tangling her hands again in his long hair, she guided his lips back to the rosy nipples of her breasts, reveling in the way he made her feel so alive, so desirable.

She felt the growing pressure deep within her as they moved together rhythmically, knew he was taking her to heights of pleasures she'd never before experienced. She moved her hands from his hair and gripped his shoulders, her movements growing more frenzied to match his. Her fingernails dug into the muscled flesh. She knew they should stop, and was deathly afraid that he would stop.

"Eve... Oh, Eve..." he groaned, his mouth trailing a blazing fire down her neck as his hands once again grabbed her buttocks and pulled her hard against him.

Dog barked. It was a short, sharp yip that made them both jump in surprise. Eve heard the dog's toenails brushing against the carpet. Then, suddenly, she found herself trapped beneath Brice as Dog laved her face with his tongue. "Ugh," she grunted, turning her head from one side to the other to escape the creature's hot breath and lavish attentions.

"Dog, no!" Brice exclaimed, pushing at the dog, who obviously thought they were playing some sort of game. Dog growled playfully, jumping on Brice's back and biting at his hair. "Damn it, Dog, I said no."

There was enough command in his voice that Dog jumped off him, sat down beside them and stared at them mournfully. "I'm sorry," Brice said, rolling off her. "I'll put him outside."

Eve shook her head and sat up, slightly dazed by the turbulent emotions still racing through her. "No, that's not necessary." Her voice sounded funny, thick and full. The moment between them had been shattered, and she knew that putting Dog outside would not recapture it.

She grabbed her bra, her face red. She suddenly felt a shyness that hadn't been there before.

"Eve?" She felt his gaze on her and looked at him, seeing the white heat that was still contained there.

She smiled regretfully, and with a small sense of relief. "It's better this way, Brice. We were both out of control, and we could have made a mistake we might have regretted."

Brice turned and looked balefully at Dog. "Stupid creature," he said scornfully. Dog seemed to shake his head in agreement.

Eve laughed shakily. "You shouldn't scold him. He has more sense than both of us put together."

"Well, his sense of timing could use some work," Brice retorted, standing up and holding out his hand to help her up off the floor. He immediately pulled her up against him. "Do you realize how crazy you make me?" he breathed against her neck, his warm breath causing a shiver that brought goose bumps to her arms.

"Brice." She pulled out of his embrace. "This is really hard for me. I want you, but I don't know where we're going." She bit her lower lip, stifling the impulse to tell him she loved him. She wouldn't say the words without knowing how he felt about her. Oh, she knew he desired her. But there was a world of difference between desiring and loving, and she refused to make a fool of herself.

He cupped her face in his hands and stared solemnly at her. Eve's heart beat fast and furious in her chest. "I don't know where this is all going, either. All I know is I won't give you false promises just to get you into bed. I can't tell you what tomorrow will bring, because I don't know what tomorrow holds. That's all I can give you right now. That's all I have to give you at this point in my life."

Eve nodded, now completely grateful for Dog's intervention. "I'm going home now," she said, moving toward the front door. "I've got some papers to grade." She also had something else she had to do. She had to figure out if what Brice was offering her was enough.

Chapter Nine

"How's this?" Eve asked Brice, pausing for his assessment of the area before spreading out the blanket for their picnic.

"It's okay, although I don't know why you insisted on a picnic at the park instead of a quiet lunch at my place," he grumbled.

Eve grinned and unfolded the large plaid blanket. "Because every time we eat at your place you insist on trying to have me for dessert."

"I can't help it if I have a voracious appetite," he protested innocently.

"Today I brought brownies for your 'voracious appetite,'" she said with a laugh.

He set the picnic basket on one end of the blanket, then stretched out on his back, patting the area next to him. "At least we're relatively alone," he conceded, scowling at a family eating at a nearby wooden table and two boys playing Frisbee in the distance. He reached for her hand as she sat down beside him. "I don't feel like I've had any real time with you for the past two weeks."

"Things have been hectic," Eve agreed. "The parent-teacher meetings toward the end of the year always throw normal routine out the window." She stretched out beside him, propping herself up on one elbow. "But you must be feeling a flush of success. I heard a lot of wonderful things from the parents."

"Overall, the comments seemed to be rather positive," he agreed.

"Rather positive? I swear, Johnny Cleavinger's mother is ready to have you proclaimed an official saint, she's so impressed with Johnny's progress."

"Hmm...at least things seem to have quieted down with Mrs. Worthington. Her camp has been unusually quiet the past two weeks."

Eve frowned. "I just hope it's not the calm before the storm."

He reached over and stroked her cheek. "It's a beautiful day. Let's not ruin it by talking about unpleasant subjects." His fingers drifted down the side of her face and across her lower lip, where they lingered. "I'd rather discuss the reasons why every time I look at you I have an overwhelming urge to kiss you."

"Gosh, I don't know. Sounds like a psychological defect to me."

He propped himself up on his elbow so that he was facing her, so close that she could feel his breath on her face. It was a tantalizing closeness that made Eve remember the night so long ago when they had come so close to making love.

"Did you know that if a man is stimulated by a woman for too long a time he can die?" If it hadn't been for the twinkle in his eyes, Eve would have thought he was dead serious.

"Oh, honestly, I heard that line for the first time when I was nineteen. I didn't believe it then, and I don't believe it now."

His eyes flickered with an emotion Eve couldn't interpret. "And what nefarious character was so bold as to use such unfair pressure on you when you were a young innocent?"

"His name was Jerry, and I met him in college. We lasted about two months, before he found another young innocent who apparently believed his line. Last I heard, he'd married her and they had three little girls."

"But you still haven't explained why I have such an insatiable hunger for you," he teased.

"Maybe you're just hungry," she answered, sitting up and grabbing the picnic basket. "And it somehow seems appropriate that I brought ham." She laughed at his look of mock outrage.

After eating lunch, neither of them was in a hurry to return home, so they lay on the blanket, talking, offering small pieces of their past, exchanging future dreams and goals. Eve shared with him her closeness with her father, and the shock and sadness of losing him. He, in turn, spoke of his loneliness and isolation in growing up the only child of parents who were much older than most.

He'd been quiet for several minutes when she looked over and realized he was sound asleep. She stared at him, enjoying the opportunity to drink her fill of him without embarrassment or self-consciousness.

A breeze whispered across them, gently playing in the dark strands of his hair. His face was boyish in sleep, finding an innocence she knew would be dispelled the moment he opened his eyes and smiled his wicked grin.

When had her heart become so full of this man? When had love surpassed the fear that had up until now given her the strength to maintain a little distance from him?

She rolled over on her back and stared up at the sun-dappled leaves of the tree above them. For the past two weeks, since the night Dog had interrupted their lovemaking, she'd spent a lot of time thinking about what Brice had said to her.

He'd made it very clear that he wasn't offering her a future. He was a man who thought only in terms of the here and now. She looked back over at his sleeping countenance, realizing that she had just about reached the point where that was enough. She loved him, and her love knew no restrictions, accepted no conditions.

It was more than just the desire he evoked in her, more than the novelty of his unconventionality. She admired his commitment to the pupils of the school, respected that he had proved himself to be an efficient administrator. She liked his sense of humor and his affectionate nature. It all added up to the fact that she loved him, and that thought no longer frightened her. She was willing to accept being a part of his life one day at a time and hope that in time he'd find that he loved her, too, and was willing to offer her a lifetime with him.

She closed her eyes, a smile lifting the corners of her mouth as she imagined a future with Brice.

Something was on her face. She jerked her head and swatted at it with the back of her hands, sighing in relief when the sensation went away. Almost immediately it was back, like a bug dancing across her cheek. She slapped at it, at the same time hearing a deep chuckle and feeling warm lips pressed against her neck.

She opened her eyes and found herself staring into his. Their warm blueness was open and vulnerable. There was no passion in his gaze, no desire to muddy the waters of his emotions. As she gazed into his eyes, what she saw was love. Her heart expanded, warming her insides like a shot of whiskey. He might not be sure of his feelings for her, but she now knew her fantasy of a future with him was based on more than just fanciful hopes.

"Ah, Sleeping Beauty awakens," he said, running his finger up and down the softness of her cheek.

"Prince Charming, I presume?" She stretched languidly and sat up, noting that the sun was now on its western descent. "How long were we asleep?"

He sat up and looked at his wristwatch. "Nearly two hours." He grinned, flashing his charming dimples. "Does this mean I can now start the rumor that I slept with you?"

She laughed. "Unfortunately, I think that particular rumor has already made the rounds." She allowed him to help her up off the blanket.

"Does it bother you?" he asked seriously, "that people are talking about us?"

"Not really. I'm finding the notoriety rather amusing." She motioned for him to pick up one end of the blanket, and she picked up the other. "We'd better be getting home. The Saturday-night bunch will be arriving before you know it."

He nodded. "They should finish up the motorcycle tonight. They've worked like demons to get it done for the auction next week."

They folded the blanket and began the walk home. Brice's hand reached out to enclose hers, his strong fingers entwining with hers.

"I can't imagine summer here," he said as they walked. "It's only May, and already it's so warm."

"This is just a mild preview of what's to come. Summers can be pretty brutal."

"What do people do here when it gets so hot?"

"What do people do in New York during the summer?" she asked.

He shrugged his broad shoulders. "Get cranky, stay inside as much as possible."

She laughed. "We must be of stronger stock here in Pawkinah. The town comes alive in the summers. We have ice-cream socials and barbecues and a huge Independence Day celebration. Then, in August, we have our Founder's Day, with an all-day country fair and a dance at night."

He squeezed her hand and smiled. "I think I'm going to like summers in Pawkinah."

And she was going to like having him here, Eve thought. She had always dreaded the coming of summer, when her mother and sister assumed that because she wasn't teaching she was at their disposal. But this summer would be different. This summer she would have a life of her own, find happiness of her own. This summer she would have Brice.

As they reached their porch, Brice set down the picnic basket and withdrew the mail from his mailbox. A frown immediately wrinkled his brow as he looked at the first envelope.

"Brice? Is something wrong?" She moved to his side and placed a hand on his arm.

"It's from Irene Worthington." He ripped open the envelope and withdrew the letter, scanning the contents quickly.

"What does it say?"

"It's an announcement of a board meeting next Saturday evening at the school." His gaze met Eve's. "It seems a decision will be reached on that night as to the question of my continued employment here in Pawkinah."

His words stole the warmth from the day and caused a fist of dread to clutch at her heart. "Oh, Brice what are you going to do?"

"I don't know," he answered simply.

Eve stood at the window of her duplex, watching the shadows of dusk lengthening to claim the last moments of daylight.

Friday night. In less than twenty-four hours, Brice's fate in Pawkinah would be decided. The past week had seemed endless. She and Brice had had little time together, and no time at all to discuss the upcoming school board meeting.

She'd heard Brice's motorcycle leave the garage a few minutes ago, rip-roaring down the street as if the hounds of hell were chasing him. She wondered if it was the same horrible feeling of helplessness she felt that had driven him to jump on his bike and take off.

If his job here ended, then she was certain he wouldn't stay. Pawkinah was so small it sported only one school. Brice was a principal. It was as much what he was as what he did. He needed a school, and if none was available here, he would move on.

Brice gone. The thought was impossible for her to accept. It was too painful. She'd gotten too close, given too much, to be able to wish him well and send him on his way.

Eve moved away from the window and paced the living room floor anxiously. If only something could be done to change Mrs. Worthington's mind. If only someone could sit down and talk to her, make her understand that the changes Brice had brought about were positive, necessary for the growth of the pupils.

She stopped pacing. Why not? Who better to talk to Mrs. Worthington than a teacher who admired Brice's work? Who better to explain his character to her than the woman who loved him? Grabbing her keys, Eve hurried to her car.

She kept her mind curiously blank as she drove to the Worthington mansion. She didn't want to sound rehearsed. Whatever she said to the woman would come from her heart.

She pulled up in the driveway and took a moment to mentally prepare herself, then marched up to the front door and knocked with an authority she didn't feel.

"Eve!" Mrs. Worthington's face registered her surprise as she opened the door.

"May I speak to you for a moment?"

"Certainly." The woman admitted Eve, leading her through the entry hall and into the library where they had held their last conversation. "Please, have a seat," Mrs. Worthington said, sitting down behind the desk.

"I'd prefer to stand," Eve replied, flushing. The woman's face once again held surprise. Eve didn't care. She needed to feel strong, and she couldn't feel that way if she was cowering in a chair.

"What can I do for you, Eve? I'm sure you aren't here for a social visit." Mrs. Worthington clasped her hands together on top of the desk and looked at Eve expectantly.

"I'm here about Brice—Mr. Maxwell," Eve began, starting to pace as she gathered her thoughts. "I think you should reconsider letting him go."

"Indeed." Her white eyebrows raised up on her forehead.

"He's a good man, a terrific principal. He sees potential in each and every child, and he's committed to pulling out that potential." She slid into the chair across from the older woman, warming to her topic. "Mrs. Worthington, I'll admit that Brice's methods are sometimes a little outlandish, but they're working. He's reaching the kids."

"Hmm...so you say," Mrs. Worthington returned doubtfully.

"Don't take my word for it," Eve exclaimed, her passions rising as she continued. "Check the records, call the parents of some of the kids." She leaned forward in the chair. "Brice has brought an electric excitement, not only to the pupils, but to most of the staff as well. He's made us care again, and isn't that better than any back-to-basics methodology that we could adopt?''

Mrs. Worthington eyed Eve sharply. "Tell me, Eve, would you be here if you weren't in love with Brice Maxwell?"

Eve sat back, shocked, her head reeling. "Is is that obvious?" she asked, with a small laugh of embarrassment.

For the first time, Irene Worthington smiled. It was a genuine, warm one that, like magic, erased some of the wrinkles on her face. "Your eyes positively sparkle every time you say his name."

Eve flushed, but held the woman's gaze proudly, defiantly. "Yes, I love Brice, but my reason for being here goes beyond that." She ran a hand distractedly through her hair. "I know change is difficult, but that doesn't make it bad. It would be nice if we could go back in time, when teachers taught the basics and didn't have to contend with other influences. But things have changed, and if our school doesn't change, our dropout rate will continue to climb and our test scores will continue to plummet. I love Brice the man, but I have enormous respect and admiration for Mr. Maxwell the principal."

"Well, that's quite a testimonial. I will certainly take into consideration everything you've said."

Eve nodded and stood up, having said everything she'd come to say.

"I must warn you," Mrs. Worthington continued, as she walked Eve to the front door, "I'm usually rather rigid once I've made up my mind."

Eve stopped at the door and grinned. "Mrs. Worthington, in the past you've been so rigid you squeak." With those words, Eve left, leaving the older woman standing at the door, her mouth agape in surprise at Eve's audaciousness.

The gymnasium was already half-full when Eve arrived at the school for the meeting the next evening. Her palms were damp, and her heart thudded with anxiety as she scanned the crowd, looking for Brice.

She spotted him standing near the podium, talking to a small group of parents. When he caught sight of her, he excused himself from the group. She watched him as he weaved his way through the crowd, pausing to greet first one person, then another. He looked proud, confident, ready for battle and ultimate victory. She envied him that. She was a basket case.

"Hi," he said, greeting her with a warm smile she knew was meant for her alone.

"Hi yourself," she replied. "My, Mr. Maxwell, you sure know how to draw a crowd." She gestured toward the front door, where people were still coming in.

"I always do my best work in front of a big audience."

"That's not what I've heard," she teased, enjoying the flash of dimples his grin evoked. She sobered and touched his arm in concern. "What's your game plan?"

"I'm going to wing it. I'm going to tell the board as openly and honestly as possible what my goals are." He paused a moment to wave across the room to someone. "However, what I'm not going to do is compromise myself or my beliefs to make one woman happy."

She nodded. She hadn't expected anything different.

"I'd better go. It looks like they're getting ready to start."

"Good luck." She squeezed his arm gently, then released it and watched as he made his way back toward the podium and the long table at the front of the room.

Within moments, the meeting got under way, Mrs. Worthington speaking from the podium and not mincing words. "As most of you know, I've called this meeting to discuss the continued employment of Mr. Brice Maxwell." A ripple of murmurs went through the crowd, causing Mrs. Worthington to bang her gavel for order. "As some of you might know, Mr. Maxwell has implemented some rather irregular programs in the last couple of weeks, programs that have caused me some doubts as to his effectiveness." Again the crowd erupted in whispers and mumbles. When it was quiet once again, Mrs. Worthington continued. "He has students going on the roof during their lunch hours, meeting at his house on the weekends. He's promised the students a dance, when he knows that the board doesn't approve of such frivolous things." She turned and looked at Brice, who sat at the far end of the table. "Perhaps, before we go any further, Mr. Maxwell would like to say a few words on his own behalf."

Brice stood up and faced the group, looking as cool and confident as Eve had ever seen him. There was a hushed silence. "I'm not going to stand up here and make a speech in my defense. I think my record speaks for itself." He sat back down.

Mrs. Worthington stood up once again. "Mr. Maxwell, I took the time this morning to look at some of the records, and I must confess I was surprised at some of the results. It seems some of your programs are effective in motivating our children, but I'm still not willing to give you a contract for next school year based on records alone. What I would like to propose to you is a sort of probation period until the end of this school year, at which time the board will decide if we wish to have you continue as principal next year. Would you agree to this?"

Brice nodded, and Eve sighed in relief. So, they weren't just arbitrarily letting him go. There was still a month of this year left, enough time for him to prove to the parents and the board that his methods, irregular or not, worked.

The moment the meeting ended, Eve made her way to where Brice stood. "I feel like I just received a stay of execution," he said.

"Thank goodness," Eve said, smiling in relief.

"Perhaps after we get out of here we can find an appropriate way to celebrate my renewed life here in Pawkinah." The light in his eyes let her know exactly what kind of celebration he had in mind.

She looked at him for a moment and realized she wanted to celebrate in the same way. She nodded with a shy smile.

Any further conversation was cut short as Mrs. Worthington joined them. "I must confess, Mr. Maxwell, up until last evening I had every intention of terminating your contract immediately."

"What made you decide differently?" he asked curiously.

The woman placed a hand on Eve's arm. "Eve did. She came to my house last evening, and we had a long discussion about you. You have quite a champion in Miss Winthrop."

"Indeed?" Brice turned and looked at Eve, his gaze suddenly cold, expressionless. *Surely it's just the bright lights overhead,* she thought, offering him a smile he didn't return. Instead, he looked back at the older woman. "Actually, I've had a few minutes now to consider your offer of a probationary term, and I've decided I don't want it. In fact, my resignation will be at your house first thing Monday morning, and you can consider it effective immediately."

Eve gasped in shock, and Mrs. Worthington sputtered in equal surprise.

"And now, if you ladies will excuse me..." He turned and headed for the gymnasium door.

"Brice?" Eve hurried after him, weaving her way through the crowd with ill-concealed impatience. But by the time she reached the parking lot, his motorcycle was gone. What had happened? Why had he suddenly resigned? She hurried to her car, needing to find him and get some answers, yet somehow afraid of what those answers might be.

Chapter Ten

Brice rode like the wind, hoping the action of riding the motorcycle hard and fast would ease the emotions that raged through him.

It had always helped in the past . . . the wind in his face, the throb of the powerful engine . . . they'd always managed to buoy his spirits in the past. But tonight was different. His spirits were at rock bottom, and after nearly an hour of riding he knew nothing was going to help.

He'd thought Eve understood him, thought she knew what was important to him, but it was obvious he had been wrong. She understood nothing, and she'd dashed any hopes he'd had of having a future in Pawkinah.

He turned the bike around, heading back to the duplex. No amount of driving would take away his feeling of betrayal. He might as well go home and write out his letter of resignation.

Moments later, he pulled up in front of the duplex and parked the bike. He walked toward the door, his footsteps slowing when he saw Eve sitting on the stoop, apparently awaiting his return.

"Brice." She stood up as he stepped up on the porch. "I've been waiting for you. We need to talk."

"Why?" he answered, fumbling with his keys, looking for the one that would open his duplex door.

"Because I need to know why you decided to resign."

He shrugged, unlocking his door and stepping inside. Before he could close it, she moved into his living room with him. He sighed. He hadn't wanted a postmortem. If she didn't understand how badly she had let him down, then they had less in common than he'd realized.

"Brice?" She placed a hand on his arm. "Please, tell me what's going on. I don't understand."

He moved away from her touch, the sense of betrayal suddenly blossoming into anger. Damn her for letting him hope that they might have a future together, and then, in one single evening, dashing those hopes to the ground and making him feel like a foolish teenager again. "Of course you don't understand," he exclaimed. "That's the whole problem."

"What are you talking about?" Eve looked genuinely puzzled, and that only fed Brice's anger with her.

He moved across the room, then turned back to stare at her, wishing he didn't still, at the very moment, want her. "I allowed you into my life more completely than I've ever allowed anyone. I told you about my problems with my parents, my needing to take control of my life. I told you I clean up my own messes. Yet, knowing all that, you did the one thing I can't forgive you for—you went to Mrs. Worthington's house and tried to clean up after me."

For a moment, Eve stared at Brice in amazement, unsure she had heard him correctly. When he'd first walked out of the gymnasium after dropping his bombshell, she'd been worried, confused, upset. But now there was an anger building in her to match his.

"You crazy fool!" She felt a certain satisfaction when he blanched at her tone. "Do you really think my intention in going to Mrs. Worthington's last night was to 'clean up after you?'" She walked over to where he stood, stopping only when she was inches from him. She studied his face intently, wishing she could see his dimples dance, wishing he was smiling one of his wicked smiles instead of staring at her with such intensity. "You're obviously carrying so much emotional baggage from your past that your judgment is sadly lacking."

She looked at him, mesmerized for a moment by the fire of anger that still blazed in his eyes. "Brice, I went to talk to Mrs. Worthington so I could clean up her mistake in firing you. I went there to support you, not to defend you.''

''There's no difference. You undermined me.'' His expression was still closed, showing that nothing she'd said so far had made any difference.

She reached out again and touched his arm. ''I went to talk to Mrs. Worthington because I love you.'' She held her breath, waiting for his response to her words. He was stunned, his expression telling her that he hadn't known how she felt about him.

Brice closed his eyes for a moment, letting her words flow like soothing balm on open wounds. God, why had she told him that? Why now, when everything was ruined? He opened his eyes and looked at her. ''And I love you, but it's not enough.'' The anger in his eyes slowly faded, and now there was only a weary resignation that frightened Eve more than the rage. ''You've been telling me all along that we're too different. I take risks, you take none. I'm impulsive, you plan everything. What you see as support, I see as defense.'' He shook his head and sighed. ''I just think it's best if I move on, find a school system that can deal with the changes I want to make, find a town that's big enough for me.''

''But what about the kids?'' she whispered. ''What about all your words of commitment?'' She could talk about the ramifications of losing him as a principal. She didn't even want to think about the loss of him in her life.

He shrugged. "They'll hire another principal—one who adheres to Mrs. Worthington's standards. The kids will survive, the teachers will survive."

But will I? Eve thought helplessly. "You're not being fair, Brice. You're letting your past interfere with your present."

"It's finished Eve. Monday morning my resignation will be on Mrs. Worthington's desk, and within a week I'll be out of here."

"Would you be quitting if it had been Margie Keller or one of the other teachers who had gone to Mrs. Worthington's last night?" she asked.

"It wasn't Margie. It was you."

"But I went there because I love you," she stressed, feeling the sting of tears burning her eyes.

"So did my parents. Every time they fixed things for me, they stole a part of my soul, and you've done the same thing." His voice was hoarse with emotion. "It's finished."

Eve didn't try to change his mind. She couldn't think of anything except escaping, getting out of there before she broke down and lost it. "By leaving, you're letting down the students and the staff, and you're letting me down. But the real sin in all of this is that you're letting yourself down." With a choking sob, she turned and ran out of his duplex and into her own.

Tears...they not only filled her eyes and dampened her pillow, but filled her heart, as well. It somehow would have been easier if he hadn't told her he loved her, too. Unreciprocated, her love would eventually have withered and faded. But knowing he loved her now made her realize the "what might have beens." And that was what made her tears spill hot and fast.

At least he had made her find laughter again. He'd helped her to settle priorities with her family and learn to give herself permission to have a life of her own. But what good was a life of her own if it didn't include him?

By morning, her grief had not subsided. In fact, it had only deepened, taking up what felt like permanent residence in her heart. There was a part of her that hoped Brice would come to his senses, realize he was turning his back on a town and a woman that could make him happy. But as she remembered the finality in his eyes, the coldness of his tone when he'd told her it was finished, she knew she was only fooling herself. He would leave, and all she would have left were memories and dreams of what might have been.

She spent the morning cleaning her place, listening for a sound from the apartment next door. It was just after noon when she heard him go out. When he was gone, she flopped down on the sofa, physically exhausted from her frenzy of cleaning and emotionally exhausted from her tears.

"Hey, Fluffy." She spoke softly to the cat, who jumped up on the couch next to her. The cat rubbed against her, as if sensing Eve's need to be loved. Eve scratched Fluffy behind her ears, her thoughts still on Brice.

She'd somehow hoped that morning would bring a new perspective on everything. She'd wanted to awaken and discover that last night had only been a bad dream—a nightmare.

Was it only last week that she'd been anxiously anticipating a summer spent with Brice? Was it only last night that they had nonverbally agreed to make love? She bit her lower lip, feeling the sting of tears once again. God, how many tears could one woman shed?

She jumped when a knock sounded at her door. Brice! Maybe he'd had time to think about everything and realized he'd overreacted to the entire situation. Maybe he'd come to tell her he would stay!

She pushed Fluffy to the floor, ignoring the feline meow of protest, and hurried to the door. She threw it open and felt her anticipation seep out of her like a balloon deflating. "Oh, it's you," she said to her sister.

"And good afternoon to you, too," Colleen exclaimed, breezing into the living room. She turned and looked at Eve. "Good grief, you look like hell!"

"I had a restless night," Eve said, sitting down on the sofa again with a weary sigh.

"I was just on my way to the bank and thought I'd stop by. Mom wants to know if you have a bundt pan she can borrow. She's having her bridge club at her house this week and thought she'd make her cherry-chocolate bundt cake."

"Sure. You know where it's at, in the cabinet next to the stove," Eve replied.

Colleen disappeared into the kitchen, returning a moment later with the pan in hand. She stood for a moment, looking at Eve curiously. Then, setting the pan on the end table, she sat down next to Eve. "Hey, sis, are you all right?"

Eve nodded. To her horror, she was afraid to speak, afraid that she would cry once again.

"Eve?" Colleen placed an arm around Eve's shoulder, and that act—her sister for the first time comforting her—made Eve realize how much Colleen had matured in the past couple of weeks. It also was the impetus that began the tears flowing again.

"Oh, Colleen, I've done something so incredibly stupid," Eve sobbed, holding on to her sister as Colleen hugged her.

"You? Eve, you never do stupid things. Remember, I'm the crazy, impetuous one in the family."

Her words caused Eve to laugh and sob at the same time. "Not this time, little sister. This time I did it. I fell in love with that crazy, brash principal who resigned last night."

Colleen untangled herself from Eve and sat back and stared at her. "Brice Maxwell? You're in love with Brice Maxwell?"

Eve nodded, sniffing indelicately and reached for a tissue from the box on the coffee table. "Stupid, huh?"

Colleen stared down at her hands, a flush of guilt on her face. "Oh, Evie, I feel horrible."

Eve swiped at her eyes and looked at her sister curiously. "Why should you feel terrible?"

"I was the one who told Mrs. Worthington about the kids coming to Brice's place every Saturday night. I sort of encouraged her to get rid of him."

"Why?" Eve looked at her sister incredulously.

Again Colleen flushed with guilt. "I was mad. Remember the day I brought back that blue dress and you made me take it to the cleaners?" Eve nodded, and Colleen continued, looking awkwardly down at her hands. "Anyway, I thought you were so mean to me, and I knew you were spending time with Brice. I thought maybe he was encouraging you to be mean to me. But, Eve, if I'd known how you felt about him, I would have never encouraged Mrs. Worthington to get rid of him." She looked at Eve, her eyes filled with misery. "I'm sorry, Eve. I really am."

Eve reached out and hugged her sister close. "It's all right, Colleen. I'm sure if it hadn't been you who helped Mrs. Worthington, somebody else would have. It was obvious from the very beginning that Brice and Mrs. Worthington would have problems with each other."

"Why did he resign?"

Eve released Colleen. "It doesn't matter. What does matter is that he did resign, and the odds are about one hundred percent that he'll be leaving Pawkinah."

"What are you going to do?" Colleen asked curiously.

Eve shrugged. "Survive." She forced a grin. "Of course, I could always stage a sit-in on top of the school, tell the news I'll stay up there until Brice agrees to withdraw his resignation."

Colleen laughed. "Nah, that's not your style." She sobered and looked at Eve. "Are you sure you'll be all right?"

"Fine," Eve answered, with more assurance than she felt.

Colleen reached over and squeezed her hand, then stood up and grabbed the bundt pan. "I guess I'd better get going. I'll check in with you later, okay?" Eve nodded.

The minute Colleen had left, Eve got up off the sofa and wandered around the room, wishing something, anything, would take her mind off Brice.

She turned when she became aware of an unfamiliar noise coming from the front of the house. Going to the window, she looked out, and then she felt her heart jump into her throat. There, on Brice's side of the driveway, was a moving van.

As she stood there, she heard the engine cut off, and she watched as Brice got out of the driver's door and went inside his apartment. Nothing spoke more eloquently of finality than the moving van parked there.

He's really leaving. The thought made a hollowness in her stomach that was so intense it ached. He's going to pack up and leave Pawkinah. The town needed him. She needed him. But he was turning his back and walking away.

She turned away from the window, running a hand through her hair. God, she couldn't stand it. She felt as fragile as a Dresden doll, afraid that she was going to shatter into a thousand pieces.

She ran a hand through her hair once again, deciding that what she needed was a good haircut. Biting her lip to keep back the tears, she went in search of the scissors.

Chapter Eleven

Brice stood at his living room window and stared out at the moving van that sat in his driveway. It have been there for almost twenty-four hours, and he had yet to pack one item.

He'd watched Eve leave for school moments before. It seemed strange for him not to be going there, as well. But he'd sent his resignation to Mrs. Worthington, and now he had no school to go to.

He turned away from the window with a heavy sigh, knowing he should be packing, but unable to summon the energy to begin the task. There was nothing to keep him here in Pawkinah, nothing except memories and unfulfilled dreams of what could have been.

He flopped down on his recliner, smiling absently as Dog ambled over and placed his big head on his lap.

He scratched the dog behind his ears, his mind whirling with unsettling thoughts.

Was he a fool? To walk away from this pleasant town, and a woman who for the first time in his life had made him consider his tomorrows? Although he had once told Eve that he had nothing to offer her but the moment, that he never thought beyond the present, he now knew that wasn't true. There was a small part of him that had been making future plans, and in those plans Eve had always been at his side.

He leaned his head back and closed his eyes, wishing he could rewrite the past three days, wishing with all his heart that Eve hadn't felt it necessary to go to Mrs. Worthington and plead his case. If only she'd let him deal with everything in his own way. If only she'd had enough faith in him to let him handle things.

Emotional baggage... Her words came back to haunt him. Was she right? Was he allowing his past to color his perceptions, interfere unnecessarily with his future? Could he walk away from here, from her?

"I'm not sure," he murmured, causing Dog to look at him curiously. "What do you think, boy?" Dog whined, and Brice felt an overwhelming need to do the same.

"Hey, Mr. Maxwell!" a voice yelled from outside the duplex.

Brice got up and went to the door, surprised to see Johnny Cleavinger standing on his front lawn. "Hi, Johnny. What are you doing out of school?"

"You've got to come to the school, Mr. Maxwell. I was sent to get you."

"Why?"

"Miss Winthrop just told me to make sure you come to the school."

Brice hesitated only a moment. Then, closing the door behind him, he joined Johnny on the sidewalk. As the two of them headed toward the school building, Brice tried to think why on earth Eve would want him there.

As they approached the school, he saw a crowd of students and staff gathered on the front lawn, and he quickened his footsteps, suddenly realizing exactly why Eve had wanted him there. He also realized why he hadn't packed. He didn't want to leave Pawkinah. He didn't want to leave Eve.

When he drew closer, his gaze automatically shot upward, and his heart exploded in his chest when he caught sight of her. She was there, up on the roof, looking as vibrant as a butterfly in a peach-colored outfit that cocooned her upper body in loving silk. A cocoon... Yes, that was what she'd been in the first time he'd seen her, wrapped in layers of self-restraint and rigid control. But she had metamorphosed, and now she was a butterfly, stretching her wings, reaching out to embrace life.

"She's gone nuts."

Brice turned to see Margie Keller standing next to him. "She looks okay to me," he replied with a grin.

"No, she's definitely lost it." Margie looked at Brice curiously. "She sent Johnny to get you, and Frankie Jenkins to get Mrs. Worthington." She looked back up at the rooftop. "She says she's not coming down until you agree to finish out this year and Mrs. Worthington rips up your resignation." Margie shook her head slowly, causing her blond curls to dance rhythmically. "Eve never does crazy, impulsive things like this. I can't imagine what's gotten into her."

Brice knew exactly what had gotten into Eve. Love. And she was showing him her love by doing something wonderfully crazy. Suddenly he realized it didn't matter why she had gone to Mrs. Worthington's. Nothing mattered, except the fact that she loved him. And, God, how he loved her.

"If you'll excuse me, Margie. Maybe I should go up there and try to talk some sense into her."

Margie slapped her forehead in disbelief. "Now I've heard everything," she exclaimed. "You talking sense into Eve!"

"Yeah, isn't love grand?" With a jaunty grin, Brice hurried to the stairs that led up to the roof and Eve.

"Don't say a word," Eve exclaimed the minute he got up there. "Please, just listen to me before you say a word."

He nodded, content for the moment just to look at her. She looked lovelier than he'd ever seen her. The peach dress clung boldly to her curves, bringing out the creaminess of her skin tones and deepening the green of her eyes. He focused his attention on her face as she began to speak.

"Brice, no matter how things stand between us personally, you can't turn your back and walk away. You've made connections here with students. You've lit a fire, and if you leave, the fire dies." Her eyes sparked with pain, and she lowered her voice as she continued. "I'm sorry if by my actions I somehow undermined you...let you down. That was never my intention. But please, don't hold my actions against the school. Stay here. Pawkinah needs you." She bit her lower lip, as if afraid to say anything more.

Brice moved over to stand in front of her. With one hand, he reached up and lightly touched her hair. "You've been wielding scissors again."

Eve ran a hand through her hair, grimacing with embarrassment. "I had a bad day yesterday."

"When we get married, are you going to try to cut my hair every time you have a bad day?"

"No, I'd never cut..." Her words trailed off, and she stared at him blankly as what he'd said slowly penetrated her mind. "Married?"

He nodded, reaching out to embrace her, and at the same time capture her lips in a kiss of burning intensity. "Oh, Eve," he murmured, "I almost made a terrible mistake. I almost didn't realize how desperately I need you in my life."

His words caused an explosion of joy to sweep through her, and she reached up and pulled his head down so that their lips could meet once again.

"We'd better plan a fast wedding," Brice said as the kiss ended.

"Why?" She tangled her hands in his hair, studying his face with a loving gaze.

He grinned, making his dimples flash entrancingly. "Because I'm still not convinced that it isn't physically dangerous to be overstimulated. And I'm definitely overstimulated every time I'm with you."

Eve smiled. "Then we'll plan a fast wedding," she agreed. "I don't want to be the cause of an early demise."

They started to kiss again, but they sprang apart when they heard footsteps clattering up the stairs. They turned to see students joining them on the roof, Johnny Cleavinger leading the parade. "Miss Winthrop, if this is a sit-in to make Mr. Maxwell stay, then we're all joining in."

As Brice and Eve watched the students kept coming until there was a large crowd gathered around them.

"Eve!"

Eve turned around, surprised to see Colleen hurrying toward her. "I was on my way to work when I heard about this little stunt of yours." She shook her head and smiled with something approaching admiration. "I can't believe you're doing this."

"I believe in Brice," Eve replied.

"I guess I'll stick around and add my support."

"But what about your job?" Eve eyed her younger sister worriedly. "When Mrs. Worthington gets here and sees you here, she may fire you."

Colleen shrugged. "If she does, it won't be the first time I've lost a job. At least this time I'll be losing it for a good reason." She smiled. "And I still think that dress would look better on me."

Eve laughed and reached out to hug her sister, grateful for her support.

"Mrs. Worthington just pulled up," a student yelled, looking over the edge of the roof.

The crowd fell silent as they all waited for the woman to make her way to the rooftop. When she got there, she made her way to where Brice and Eve stood.

"Good morning," she said. She looked around at the crowd that surrounded them. "You two certainly know how to form a mob."

"Mrs. Worthington, we're up here to show our support for Mr. Maxwell. We don't want him to resign. We want him to finish out this year and have a contract for next year." Eve hesitated, then added, "With no probationary time."

There was a long moment of silence. "And this is what you want?" Mrs. Worthington asked Brice.

He nodded, watching as she opened her purse and withdrew a sheet of paper he recognized as his resignation. "So, I assume you want me to rip this up?" Again he nodded.

She sighed and looked at the group of kids, who had been watching silently. "I was told quite recently that there are times when I'm so rigid I squeak." She looked at Eve, who colored slightly, then back at Brice. "You realize there will be times when you'll think I'm terribly rigid."

"And I'm sure there will be times when you think I'm completely nuts," he returned with a small smile.

"We'll probably fight, and you won't always win."

Brice grinned widely. "But neither will you."

Mrs. Worthington laughed. "You are quite impertinent, Mr. Maxwell."

"Yes, ma'am."

"But you seem to inspire a large amount of loyalty among the people you work with. You must be doing something right." She looked at him for another long moment, then ripped his resignation letter in two. "I'll have new contracts sent to you this afternoon." She gestured to the students. "Don't you think you'd better get these children off this roof and into the classrooms? After all, Mr. Maxwell, you have a school to run."

She turned and headed for the stairs, pausing before she began her descent. "Colleen, are you coming? We have a lot of work to accomplish today." Without waiting for a reply, she disappeared down the stairs, Colleen scurrying after her.

The moment they were gone, a cheer went up from the kids. "Okay, gang," Brice yelled, quieting the crowd. "Back to class. You heard Mrs. Worthington. We have a school to run."

It only took a few minutes for the roof to empty of everyone except Brice and Eve. "Now where were we before we were so rudely interrupted?" he asked, pulling her into his arms.

"I think we'd just agreed to have a quick wedding," Eve replied, molding her body against his, loving the way they fit together so perfectly.

"I love you, Eve," he said, his azure eyes speaking the emotion.

"And I love you," she returned, the fullness of her heart bringing tears to her eyes. "You asked me one time if I needed a man like you in my life and I didn't answer you. I do, Brice. Pawkinah needs you, but I need you more."

His lips claimed hers in a tender kiss that held the promise of forever. When their lips finally parted, he sighed regretfully. "I suppose we really should get to work."

"Yes, we should." Together they walked toward the stairs. Before she began to climb down, Brice stopped her.

"Eve, have you ever spent a wedding night making love in a bathtub full of bubbles?" His wicked smile danced on his lips.

"No." She laughed. "But I have a feeling it's in my future."

"The very near future," he replied, causing a shiver of anticipation to rush through her.

"If you don't stop looking at me like that, I'm going to be the first female to die from overstimulation," she whispered breathlessly.

With an exuberant laugh, Brice grabbed her hand, and together they left the rooftop, knowing the future lay just ahead.

Epilogue

"Happy is the bride that the sun shines on," Colleen exclaimed as she walked into the classroom Eve had been using as a dressing area.

Eve smiled nervously at her sister. "I half expected a hurricane or a tornado. I can't imagine Brice allowing our wedding to take place on a normal, unexciting summer day."

"One thing is for sure, when Brice Maxwell blew into town he brought with him a pocketful of excitement," Colleen agreed, with a wide grin. "The gossipmongers in this town have never had it so good."

Eve nodded and turned back to face the mirror, nervously checking her reflection one last time. Thank goodness she hadn't reached for a pair of scissors in a nervous frenzy earlier that morning. Her hair had finally grown out of the punky spike and now lay neatly beneath the pearl-encrusted cap and veil.

The dress itself was beautiful, and conventional, with its layers of lace and its high-necked collar. Brice had teasingly dared her to wear a mini-length wedding dress, but Eve had clung to her old-fashioned values and chosen this traditional gown.

Brice... Her heart skipped a beat as she realized that in less than an hour she would be his wife. Who would have thought when that wildly sexy leather-clad man had shown up by mistake at her door that their lives would intertwine like flowering vines?

In the past two months, since the day of his proposal, they'd been on a whirlwind of happiness, riding the crest of a wave of love so great it was at times dizzying. There had been arguments, good-natured fights prompted by Brice's unpredictableness and her own desire to cling to the status quo, but each argument had ended with a compromise and a kiss, and she had a feeling that would be the basis of their marriage.

She turned and looked at Colleen, who looked as pretty as a flower in her pale blue maid of honor's gown. "Do I look all right?" she asked the younger girl worriedly.

"Oh, Eve, you look beautiful." Colleen hugged her. "And I saw your groom a few minutes ago, and he looks absolutely magnificent."

"He wasn't wearing a leather jacket or anything like that?" Eve asked anxiously.

Colleen giggled and shook her head. "No, no leather jacket, although I wasn't crazy about the beads in his hair." She laughed again at Eve's stricken look. "Just kidding... Actually, he looked just like any other groom. Gorgeous in his tux, and nervous as hell." Colleen smoothed the side of Eve's dress. "The gym is nearly full."

Eve nodded. They'd expected a big crowd. All the students had wanted to attend the wedding, so Brice had thought it best that they marry in the school gymnasium, where seating wouldn't be a problem for anyone who wanted to come.

Her stomach quivered nervously as she thought of a whole gym full of people. Maybe it would have been better had they eloped. She immediately dismissed the idea. Brice's relationship with the students was part of what she loved about him, and he'd thought it was important that the kids have an active role in the wedding. They'd been busy all week making paper flowers, decorating the gym, making it appropriate for a wedding ceremony.

Somebody rapped on the door and called, "It's time."

Eve immediately looked at Colleen in panic. Colleen hugged her once again. "You'll be fine, sis," the younger girl said. "You've got to do this right so I'll know how to do it when it's my turn."

Minutes later, Eve stood alone at the back of the gym, watching her wedding procession taking place. The gym had been transformed into a chapel of love.

Paper flowers were everywhere, hanging from the walls, woven together to form chains, littering the floor. The students had even suspended a mirrored ball from the ceiling, and it sparkled, sending out shooting starlight that lent the room a magical aura.

As the wedding march reached its height, she began her walk across the polished floor, hearing the hush that fell over the crowd. Her gaze focused on Brice, who stood tall and handsome, his eyes filled with a depth of emotion that stole her breath away.

She'd almost reached his side when she realized who sat next to him. At his side, a ribbon tied to his mangled ear, sat Dog, looking uglier than ever, and pleased to be part of the excitement. Clutched in his mouth was the ring-bearer's pillow, their wedding bands tied to it with a ribbon.

All Eve's fears, all her doubts, melted away as laughter bubbled up inside her. Oh, yes, this man of hers had brought a pocketful of excitement with him when he'd breezed into town. He'd also brought something new, something wonderful into her life...something called love....

* * * * *

SMYTHESHIRE,
MASSACHUSETTS.

Small town. Big secrets.

**Silhouette Romance invites you to visit Elizabeth August's
intriguing small town, a place with an unusual legacy
rooted deep in the past....**

**THE VIRGIN WIFE (#921) February 1993
HAUNTED HUSBAND (#922) March 1993
LUCKY PENNY (#945) June 1993
A WEDDING FOR EMILY (#953) August 1993**

Elizabeth August's SMYTHESHIRE, MASSACHUSETTS—
This sleepy little town has plenty to keep you up at night.
Only from Silhouette Romance!

WHERE WERE YOU WHEN THE LIGHTS WENT OUT?

S I L H O U E T T E

SUMMER
Sizzlers
'93

This summer, Silhouette turns up the heat when a midsummer blackout leaves the entire Eastern seaboard in the dark. Who could ask for a more romantic atmosphere? And who can deliver it better than:

LINDA HOWARD
CAROLE BUCK
SUZANNE CAREY

Look for it this June at your favorite retail outlet.

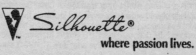

Silhouette®

where passion lives.

Wedding bells ring in our celebration of love and marriage. And *You're Invited!* Be our guest as five special couples find the magic ingredients for happily-wed-ever-afters! Look for these wonderful stories by some of your favorite authors...

Something Old—Toni Collins #941
Adrian Lacross was handsome and so romantic. How could Gabriella Thorne resist? If only he wasn't...a vampire! Could Gabriella's love make Adrian a new man?

Something New—Carla Cassidy #942
Eve Winthrop was shocked when the new principal showed up on a motorcycle. But Brice Maxwell dared to shake up his new students—and to take Eve for a ride on the wild side.

Something Borrowed—Linda Varner #943
Brooke Brady was on the yellow brick road to a new life when a tornado blew her car onto Patrick Sawyer's property. Was Patrick a heartless Tin Man—or a misunderstood Wizard?

Something Blue—Jayne Addison #944
Newly divorced, Quinn Barnett and Tony Falco found they were going to share more than memories—parenthood. Their baby seemed a miracle—and a message to give love another chance.

Lucky Penny—Elizabeth August #945
Dr. Reid Prescott didn't want love, but he needed a wife. Celina Warley was single and longed for a child. They weren't looking for vows of love...but with luck, would love find them?

WED-A

Is your father a Fabulous Father?

Then enter him in Silhouette Romance's

"FATHER OF THE YEAR" Contest
and you can both win some great prizes! Look for contest details
in the FABULOUS FATHER titles available in June, July
and August...

ONE MAN'S VOW by Diana Whitney
Available in June

ACCIDENTAL DAD by Anne Peters
Available in July

INSTANT FATHER by Lucy Gordon
Available in August

Only from